John Leith

Leith's narrative : a short biography with a brief account of

his life among the Indians

John Leith

Leith's narrative : a short biography with a brief account of his life among the Indians

ISBN/EAN: 9783337304829

Printed in Europe, USA, Canada, Australia, Japan

Cover: Foto ©Andreas Hilbeck / pixelio.de

More available books at **www.hansebooks.com**

LEITH'S NARRATIVE

A

SHORT BIOGRAPHY

OF

JOHN LEITH

*WITH A BRIEF ACCOUNT OF HIS LIFE AMONG
THE INDIANS*

A REPRINT

WITH ILLUSTRATIVE NOTES

BY

C. W. BUTTERFIELD

Author of " Nicolet's Discovery of the Northwest," " Washington-Irvine
Correspondence," and other works

CINCINNATI
ROBERT CLARKE & CO
1883

PREFATORY.

In adding illustrative notes to this reprint, the object has been to make the story more intelligible to the general reader; for, as it stands originally, even the critical student of western history, without considerable thought and study, might fail to realize its importance. The annotations begin with Leith's introduction to savage life, and end with his final return to civilization; beyond this point, the narrative gives a vivid portrayal of hardships and privations such as were incident to the early settlement of the West; but the recital needs little if any elucidation, and none is given.

This narrative, considering the age of the narrator when it was taken from his lips, and the number of years which had elapsed since he bade adieu to Indian haunts, is unusually accurate. What few errors in his statements have been discovered, are pointed out in the foot-notes. The mistake in spelling Leith's name is clearly traceable to his editor, as the same orthography is adopted when the city of Leith, Scotland, is mentioned,—it being given " Leeth." The spelling, punctuation, and capitalization of the original are strictly followed in the reprint; and the original paging is indicated therein by brackets. Adding greatly to the understanding of Leith's relation of events in the wilderness are the depositions given by him immediately after the occurrence of some of them. It is only recently that one of these valuable contemporaneous statements has been brought to light. The republication of what has become so excessively rare as this pamphlet, in a measure rescues from oblivion a valuable contribution to American history, especially to that portion of it relating to the region of the Northwest.

C. W. B.

Madison, Wis., *January*, 1883.

A
SHORT BIOGRAPHY

OF

JOHN LEETH,

GIVING A BRIEF ACCOUNT OF HIS TRAVELS AND SUFFER-
INGS AMONG THE

Indians for eighteen years,

TOGETHER WITH

HIS RELIGIOUS EXERCISES,

FROM HIS OWN RELATION,

BY EWEL JEFFRIES.

LANCASTER, OHIO.
PRINTED AT THE GAZETTE OFFICE—MAIN ST.
1831.

PREFACE.

The design of the following work is to show the providence of God, in guiding his creatures through life, although their situation, at times, may be, to all appearance, dismaying, perilous and almost insurmountable.

Mr. LEETH, the subject of the following pages, is now living [1831], and has long been a respectable member of the Methodist Communion. Having been directed, by an unseen hand, through all the vicissitudes of fortune, from the savage haunts of a boundless wilderness, to the peaceful shades of civilized society, with a competency to make his declining years easy and respectable, in the large circle of friends in which he moves, he may truly say, the Christian's life is a life of pleasantness.

THE AUTHOR.

Biography of John Leeth.

I was born in Hickory Grove, on the Pedee River, South Carolina, on the 15th day of March, 1755, of respectable parents, though of low circumstances in the world. My father died before I was born; and my mother died when I was about five years of age; after which, I was bound to a Tailor to learn the trade. Shortly after I had entered into my new situation, my master removed to Charleston, S. C. and took me with him. After I had remained in his family about two years, my mind became restless; and I eloped from my master and his service. I made my way for Little York, in Pennsylvania; and when I arrived there, I came to the conclusion that I was not properly able to take care of myself, and bound myself to a farmer for the term of four years; which time I served out with becoming fortitude and agility. [When my time of service was out, and I was free from my master, I bent my course to Fort Pitt now Pittsburg;[1] and hired

---

[1] A fort—Duquesne—was built at the point in the forks of the Alleghany and Monongahela rivers where they form the Ohio, by

myself to an Indian trader. Our first rout, from

the French at the commencement of the old French war, but was
burned by them in 1758, immediately before the occupation of
the place by the British, under General Forbes. It was a strong
fortification of earth and wood stockaded. In December, 1758,
the British erected a small stockade, with bastions, within two
hundred yards of the ruins of the French post. The next year,
however, was commenced a more formidable fortification. It was
near the site of Fort Duquesne, and was named Fort Pitt. It remained in possession of a British force until the latter part of the
year 1772, when it was abandoned and considerably, though not
wholly, destroyed. During the year 1773, a citizen of Pittsburgh—
Edward Ward—had possession of what was left. It was, in
1774, reoccupied and somewhat repaired by Captain John Conolly, under orders from Lord Dunmore, as a Virginia post, and
its name changed to Fort Dunmore, though the Pennsylvanians
still adhered to " Fort Pitt," which name was fully restored when
Dunmore became odious to Virginia. It was vacated by Conolly
just at the commencement of the Revolution. Its first occupation
after that struggle began was by Virginia troops under Captain
John Neville, in 1775, who were superceded early in 1777 by
others raised in the immediate neighborhood. Following these
was a continental garrison, first under Brigadier-General Edward Hand, afterward under Brigadier-General Lachlan Mc-
Intosh, whose successor was Colonel Daniel Brodhead, followed by Colonel John Gibson, the latter being succeeded by
Brigadier-General William Irvine, who remained in command
until October 1, 1783. The post was then put under the charge
of Captain Joseph Marbury, who occupied it with a small
force for a brief season. His successor was Lieutenant D.
Luckett; the latter turned it over to Lieutenant-Colonel Josiah

thence, was to New Lancaster, (then an Indian Town,) in the State of Ohio;[1] and after being there some

---

Harmar, and it became little else than a government storehouse from this time on to its final abandonment.

The words "now Pittsburg" imply that, at the time of Leith's arrival at Fort Pitt, there was no town known as Pittsburgh there; but this is erroneous, as a "burgh" thus named had had an existence at that point quite as long as the fort. A writer, speaking of both at about the date of Leith's reaching Fort Pitt, says:

"At this time [June, 1772] the fortification [Fort Pitt] was remaining, but somewhat impaired. Here were about eighty soldiers, with one commanding officer. It is said the erecting of this fort cost the Crown £100,000 sterling; by some orders in the fall, it was demolished and abandoned. East at about two hundred yards distance, by the Monongahela, there is a small town [Pittsburgh], chiefly inhabited by Indian traders and some mechanics. The army was without a chaplain, nor was the town supplied with any minister. Part of the inhabitants are agreeable and worthy of regard, while others are lamentably dissolute in their morals."—Jones' *Journal*, p. 20. Such was Pittsburgh one hundred and ten years ago.

[1] It would have been nearer correct had he said "the present Lancaster (then an Indian town called the Standing Stone, in English), in what is now the State of Ohio."

In the fall of 1800, Ebenezer Zane laid out a town on the Hockhocking river, in what is now Fairfield county, O., to which he gave the name of New Lancaster. It retained that name legally until 1805, when, by an act of the legislature, the word "New" was dropped; but the place continued to be called by its original name long after by the early settlers. Near by stands a

length of time, in his employ, having the care and oversight of his goods, I was taken prisoner by the Delaware Indians,[1] in the following manner, when about seventeen years of age:—On the 10th day of April, 1772,[2] when my employer had been from home

bold eminence, which, at an early day, gave the name of the Standing Stone to a Delaware Indian village located there.

The Rev. David Jones was here on Tuesday, February 9, 1773. He says: " Before nine o'clock, came safe to Mr. McCormick's, at the Standing Stone. This town consists chiefly of Delaware Indians. It is situated on a creek called Hockhocking. The soil about this [place] is equal to the highest wishes, but the creek appears muddy. Though it is not wide, yet it soon admits large canoes, and from hence peltry is transmitted to Fort Pitt. Overtook here Mr. David Duncan, a trader from Shippen's town, who was going to Fort Pitt."—Jones' *Journal*, p. 86.

Lancaster (as it is now called), the capital of Fairfield county, Ohio, is situated on the Hocking river and the Hocking canal, thirty-two miles southeast of Columbus, one hundred and sixteen miles east northeast of Cincinnati, and fifty-two miles west southwest of Zanesville. It is on the Columbus and Hocking Valley railroad where it crosses the Cincinnati and Muskingum Valley railroad.

[1] The Standing Stone (now Lancaster, Ohio,) was the farthest town to the southwest inhabited by Delaware Indians at this date. From this point northeast was Delaware territory (as claimed by that tribe) well up to Pittsburgh. Their principal town was Coshocton, on the Muskingum river, the site of the town of that name, county-seat of Coshocton county, Ohio.

[2] This date is incorrect, as shown by what follows. The year was 1774.

two weeks, I was lying on some skins in my employer's store; an Indian boy came to me, and told [6] me his father wanted to see me. I went with him; and when I came to the old man, he showed me a place to sit down. I took my seat with much wonder and surprise. As I could not yet understand Indian language, the old Indian having a white woman for his wife,[1] made her interpreter for us. [He began with asking me if I had heard the news that a war had broken out between the whites and Indians; that the Shawnees[2] had killed seven white men, and taken four prisoners;[3] that the Virginians had taken Mingo Town, at Cross

[1] By this it will be seen that two years before the commencement of the Revolution, what is now Lancaster, Ohio, had at least one white resident who was not a trader. Of her history, nothing whatever is known.

[2] The Shawanese, in 1774, had their homes in a number of villages upon the waters of the Scioto river and beyond, in what is now the State of Ohio; but there were outlying towns of theirs to the eastward as far as the Muskingum below Coshocton. The "Pickaway plains" may be considered as having been, at that date, about the center of their territory.

[3] It is now impossible to say exactly what act of hostility is here referred to as being the first on the list of those resulting in what is known as Lord Dunmore's war. But the importance of the statement consists in the assertion that the Shawanese were the aggressors—the first to commence the work of death.

Creek, on the Ohio River.[1] I answered him, that I had heard nothing of it. He asked me what I thought of the matter. With a trembling heart I informed him, I knew not what to think of it; that I had never done them any harm; I had no hand in the matter, and hoped they would take care of me. He then told me to rise and stand up on my feet. With the fearful expectation he intended to kill me immediately, I arose, and stood before him. He then proceeded,—"Your mother has risen from the dead to give you suck;" at the same time pointing to his wife's breast; then laid his hand on his own breast, and said,—"Your father has also arisen to take care of you, and you need not be afraid, for I will be a father to you." He then embraced my neck, and called the chiefs around him; when they proceeded to divide the store-goods, spirits, and all that I had care of, among themselves.[2]

[1] The Mingo town mentioned above was on what was known as the Mingo bottom, just below the present Steuben-ville, Jefferson county, Ohio. The town was not taken by the Virginians as the Delaware chief supposed; but the Mingoes, immediately after the killing of Logan's relatives and other Indians, opposite the mouth of Yellow creek, on the 30th of April, 1774, by Greathouse and party, left the Ohio river never to return.]

[2] This fact has an important bearing upon the question as to the disposition of the Delawares towards the white traders, at the first report of war existing between the Shawanese and

The same fall, General Dunmore,[1] a British officer, came out against the Indians, with a considerable army of whites;[2] and after a variety of skirmishing and manœuvreing, a decisive battle was fought at the

Mingoes on the one side and the Virginians on the other. The Delawares as a tribe were not drawn into the conflict. The confiscation of the goods belonging to the trader at the Standing Stone, in care of Leith, would probably not have taken place in any other of the Delaware villages; but there Shawanese influence was predominant.

[1] John Murray, 4th Earl of Dunmore, one of the representative peers of Scotland, was, at that date, governor of Virginia.

[2] In July, 1774, Major Angus McDonald arrived over the mountains with a considerable force of Virginia militia, which, when embodied with those already raised in the West, amounted to seven hundred men. McDonald went down the Ohio as far as Wheeling, in order to take command, as there the whole force rendezvoused. A stockade fort (Fort Fincastle) was erected under the joint directions of Major McDonald and Captain William Crawford.

On the 26th of July, about four hundred men, having left Wheeling, arrived at the mouth of Fish creek, on the east side of the Ohio, twenty-four miles below. Here they determined to move against the Shawanese villages upon the Muskingum river, in what is now Muskingum county, Ohio. The men were led by Major McDonald. Captain Crawford remained in command at Fort Fincastle. The expedition proved successful. Wakatomica (near what is now Dresden, Ohio,) and other Shawanese towns were destroyed, and con-

mouth of the Big Kenhawa;[1] the Indians retreated
with the loss of about twenty-five; the army pursued
and overtook them while they were crossing the river,
and killed about twenty-five more; after which the
Indians returned to their habitations, and gave up
the contest for that time.[2] Some time after, news

---

siderable plunder secured. This was the first effective blow
struck by Virginia troops in Lord Dunmore's war.

Lord Dunmore left Williamsburg, Virginia, July 10, 1774,
for the frontiers, reaching Fredericksburg on the 15th and Win-
chester some days after. Here he remained some time, to get
in order as many men as possible for service against the savages.
Such as were raised in the counties of Frederick, Berkeley,
and Dunmore were put under the command of Adam Stephen
as colonel. About the end of August they marched for Pittsburgh, accompanied by his Lordship. On the last day of
September, Dunmore reached Wheeling with twelve hundred
men. Major (previously Captain) Crawford, with five hundred,
was sent in advance to the mouth of the Hocking river, where
he commenced the erection of a stockade, which received the
name of Fort Gower, Dunmore arriving with the residue of
his men in time to take part in its construction. Here we will
leave him for the present.

[1] By Big Kenhawa is meant the river now known as the
Great Kanawha.

[2] Before Dunmore left Williamsburg he had authorized Colonel Andrew Lewis to march an army down this river to its
mouth, there to erect a fort; and then if he thought proper to
attack the hostile towns of the savages beyond the Ohio. Lewis
reached his point of destination, where he was unexpectedly
attacked by the Indians (Shawanese, Mingoes, and some from

came that Dunmore was marching up the Hockhocking Ri[7]ver,[1] with an army;[2] when some of the

other tribes) on the 10th of October. A battle ensued which
lasted till nightfall. Lewis claimed the victory, but suffered
severely in killed and wounded. This is the conflict known
in history as the battle of Point Pleasant.

[1] Hocking river, Ohio, rises in Fairfield county, runs southeastward through Hocking and Athens counties, and enters
the Ohio river about fourteen miles below Parkersburg, West
Virginia. The chief towns on its banks are Lancaster, Logan,
and Athens. It traverses the Ohio coal-field.

[2] In a previous note we left Lord Dunmore with his army
at the mouth of the Hocking river assisting Captain Crawford
in finishing "Fort Gower." At that time his Lordship was
ignorant as to whether Colonel Andrew Lewis with his men
had reached the Ohio, a message sent by Dunmore having
arrived at the mouth of the Great Kanawha in advance of that
officer. Another express was thereupon dispatched, which, on
the 8th of October, 1774, found Lewis at Point Pleasant—the
name of the place in the forks of the Great Kanawha and the
Ohio. His orders were to march up the Ohio and join Dunmore at the mouth of the Hocking. Meanwhile scouts had
been sent by him to Dunmore. These returned to Point Pleasant on the 13th of October, three days after the battle there,
with an order from his Lordship (who was ignorant of what
had taken place between Lewis' force and the savages) to march
directly toward the Shawanese towns upon the Scioto, and join
him at a certain point on the way.

Lord Dunmore now put his division in motion up the Hocking river for the same destination to which Lewis had been
ordered, namely, the Shawanese towns. It was just at this time

Indians proposed to kill me, and put me out of the
way; but my late father, (for he was a father to me indeed,) interfered, and prevented their horrid intention.
They then commenced their flight from the Towns, and
took me with them, with my hands bound behind my
back ; they took me a long and wearisome journey to
their camp.[1] Before we arrived at the camp, I formed
a firm and settled resolution to make my escape,
if any opportunity should offer, at which I made
several attempts ; but was so closely watched, that all
possibility of an escape was utterly abortive. General
Dunmore marched to Shawnee Town, where Chillicothe now is,[2] where he received a letter informing him
that war was proclaimed ; and not thinking himself safe
in the situation he was, in order to make his escape,

---

that news was received upon the Scioto by the Indians, as related by Leith, of the advance of Dunmore up the "Hockhocking river with an army."

[1] Their camp was doubtless some one of the Shawanese villages upon the waters either of the Little Miami or Great Miami
river, in what is now the State of Ohio.

[2] Our last mention of Dunmore was to the effect that both
divisions of his army were marching for the Shawanese towns,—
he by way of the Hocking river, and Lewis across from the
mouth of the Great Kanawha. His Lordship was overtaken on
his march by a courier from Lewis, informing him of the hard-
fought battle with the Shawanese and Mingoes at Point Pleasant,
on the 10th of October. On the 17th, Lewis crossed the Ohio,
and, agreeably to orders, marched directly for the Scioto to join

made a pretended peace with the Indians.[1] After the
cessation of hostilities, my father gave me and his two
sons our freedom, with a rifle, two pounds of powder,
four pounds of lead, a blanket, shirt, match-coat, pair
of leggins, &c. to each, as our freedom suits; and told
us to shift for ourselves. Having my freedom to act
for myself, but destined to remain in an uncultivated
wilderness, where no voice was heard but the yells of
savages, the howling of wolves, and the dread screams of

Dunmore. A junction of the two forces occurred before the
Scioto was actually reached, under circumstances soon to be
related.

Leith's idea was that Lord Dunmore actually reached the spot
now the site of the city of Chillicothe, Ohio, then one of the
Shawanese towns; but such was not the fact. His Lordship was
met, before he reached the Indian villages, with a deputation from
the enemy anxious for an accommodation. A treaty was held at
"Camp Charlotte," in what is now Pickaway county, Ohio,—some
of the Shawanese villages being in the immediate vicinity; but
the arrival of Lewis and his gallant troops, fresh from the red
field of conflict at Point Pleasant, breathing revenge against the
savages, was an element difficult to be controlled by Dunmore.
However, no order was intentionally disobeyed by Lewis, who
was commanded to return with his division to the mouth of the
Great Kanawha.

[1] Leith's information was singularly inaccurate as to the peace
entered into between Dunmore and the Indians. He (Leith) was
not present at "Camp Charlotte" at the time, having been taken
a considerable distance to the westward, as is just before explained
by himself. The treaty was dictated to the Shawanese and Min-

the panther; no cultivated fields or lowing herds, nor any prospect for the support of life, but what the dreary regions of a wide and boundless wilderness presented, was appalling and discouraging;[1] and what added horror to my situation was, it was death to make an attempt at seeking a more hospitable and fruitful clime : However, Providence smiled on me, and I made my living by hunting, and trading with the Indians. In the course of about two years, I had accumulated a considerable

goes by Dunmore; for a peace had already been conquered by the Virginians at a sacrifice of many valuable lives, at Point Pleasant.

The stipulations were that the Shawanese and Mingoes were to give up all the prisoners ever taken by them in war with the white people still remaining in their possession or living with them ; also, all negroes and all the horses stolen or taken by them since the last war. And, further, no Indian was, for the future, to hunt on the east side of the Ohio, nor any white man on the west side. As a guarantee, on the part of the savages, of the fulfillment of their agreement, they were to give up four of their chief men as hostages, who were to be relieved yearly, or as they might choose. It was also arranged that a supplemental treaty should be held the ensuing spring at Pittsburgh. However, the Mingoes were not brought fully to terms until their towns in what is now Franklin county, Ohio, had been destroyed by a detachment sent against them by his Lordship under Major William Crawford. With hostages to insure the fulfillment of the stipulations of the treaty, Dunmore retraced his steps down the Hocking river ; and the war was ended.

[1] This rhetorical flourish is probably to be charged up to Mr. Jeffries.

property in skins, furs, &c. perhaps to the amount of two or three hundred dollars, spending my time mostly in some useful employment.[1]

About two years from the time of my freedom, about twenty Indians came from another tribe; and while I [8] was dealing with a trader and his assistant, took us all prisoners with all our property. They took me a considerable rout through the wilderness; and after some days sold me to another nation of Indians.[2] Soon after I was sold, my purchaser informed me he did not buy me for the purpose of enslaving me; it was only because he loved me and wished me to stay with him; and gave my liberty on my promise not to leave him.[3] At that time I had nothing but my gun. I then set out once more to shift for myself in the woods; and by hunting and trading that fall and spring,[4] accumulated furs and skins to the amount of seventy or seventy-five dollars.[5]

---

[1] Although the narrator was free to act for himself, his connection with the Delawares had by no means ceased.

[2] The narrative is here provokingly silent as to the names of the two tribes who had, in succession, their white prisoner with them. Certain circumstances induce the belief that the first mentioned was the Shawanese tribe; the other, the Wyandot.

[3] This declaration of Leith's purchaser certainly exhibits that savage in a very amiable light.

[4] This was in the spring of 1777.

[5] It seems that, among other places visited by Leith, the valley of the Vernon river, in what is now the central part of the State

About this time, the war between Great Britain and America,[1] with their Indian allies,[2] was at its height. I went with some of the Indian traders to Detroit;[3] and when we arrived there, the British had the command and control of the place, furnishing the Indians with fire-arms, ammunition, the tomahawk and scalping-knife, to assist them against the whites of America. Having by this time become perfectly acquainted with the Indian language,[4] and inured to their habits and customs, I then engaged with an Indian trader, who was to pay me

of Ohio, was one of his favorite hunting-grounds during this period.

During the summer of 1825, Mr. Leith visited the family of Lyman W. Gates' father in Knox county, Ohio, and spent some time there. Wishing to visit Mt. Vernon, the county-seat of that county, Mr. Gates' father accompanied him. When they had reached the Gotshall place, Mr. Leith got off his horse, and pointed out the places where he had lain in wait for the wild animals to come and drink, and where he shot them. He also pointed out other localities along the road where he had hunted successfully.

Vernon river rises in the present county of Morrow, Ohio, runs eastward through Knox county, and enters the Mohican (or Walhonding) river, in the western part of Coshocton county.

[1] Meaning, of course, the Revolution.

[2] That is, the war of Great Britain and her Indian allies with America, was, etc.

[3] This was in the year 1777. Detroit was identical with the site of the present city of that name, the metropolis of Michigan.

[4] Leith means evidently the Wyandot language. He could, of course, speak the Delaware also, and probably the Shawanese.

seven pounds ten shillings per month, with victuals and
clothing exclusively.[1] After engaging me, my employer
returned to Sandusky,[2] where he had been a considerable
time engaged, leaving his goods with me to take on by
water, across the Lake. Fort Detroit was then under
martial law,[3] and no person was permitted to go in or
out without a pass from the Governor[4] thereof. When

[1] The word "exclusively" is here used in the sense of "included." It is subsequently employed in this narrative, having the
same meaning. The trader's name was Arundle.

[2] Lower Sandusky, now the site of Fremont, in Sandusky
county, Ohio.

The Sandusky river, on which Lower Sandusky was situated,
rises in Springfield township, Richland county, Ohio, flowing a
southwesterly course, through Crawford county, passing into
Wyandot county, a little over two miles north of the southeast
corner. Soon after it sweeps around to the northward, and, following generally a northerly direction through that county,
enters Seneca county. It pursues the same general course
through Seneca and Sandusky counties, falling into the head of
Sandusky bay about eighty miles, by the course of the stream,
from its source.

[3] There were then in the fort four companies of the Eighth (or
King's) regiment, commanded by Captain (afterward Major) R.
B. Lernoult; two companies of Butler's Rangers, commanded by
Captain William Caldwell, and one company of the Forty-seventh
regiment, commanded by Captain Thomas Aubrey. The British
also had a small navy, which commanded the lakes. There were,
usually, several hundred Indians gathered about the fort.

[4] Under the Quebec act of 1774, Colonel Henry Hamilton,
formerly a captain in the Fifteenth regiment, was appointed by

I had made my arrangements to start with the goods, I went to the Governor for a pass, informing him my employer had left orders with me to follow on after him, with the goods. He asked where I wanted to take them. I told him to Sandusky. He then asked me what my employer gave me per month. I told him. He said it was not enough, and if I would join the Indian department under his command, he would give me two

Governor Carlton, in 1775, "Lieutenant-Governor and Superintendent of Detroit and its Dependencies," including the entire Northwest. He had doubtless been selected because of his capacity, energy, and zeal, and with reference to the impending difficulties between the colonies and the mother country. Henceforth, and during the entire Revolution, Detroit was the center of British power in the Northwest. The relentless and cruel Indian warfare that was carried on against the border settlements of Pennsylvania, Virginia, and Kentucky received its inspiration and direction from this point.

In the latter part of winter, or early in the spring of that year (that is, 1777), Governor Hamilton sent a war hatchet, wrapped in a belt of red and white beads, to the Ohio Indians. It was accepted by the Wyandots and Shawanese, but rejected by the Delawares. Its effect was at once apparent. On the 6th of March, a large party of Indians appeared before Harrodsburgh, in Kentucky. On the 24th of April, Boonsborough was attacked, and again on the 23d of May; and, on the 30th of May, Logan's fort. On the 27th of July, Hamilton reported to Secretary Germaine that he had already sent out fifteen several parties of Indians, consisting of two hundred and eighty-nine braves, with thirty white officers and rangers, to prowl on the frontiers of Pennsylvania and Virginia.

dollars per [9] day,[1] and one and a half rations exclusively.[2] I then asked him what he wanted me to do.
He answered, he wanted me to interpret for them, and
sometimes go to war with them, against their enemies;[3]
observing, as I understood both languages,[4] I would be

[1] The following was the pay of " Officers, Inspectors, Smiths,
etc., in the Indian Department at Detroit, October 24, 1779:"
Duperon Baby, Alexander McKee, Isadore Chêne, Charles Beau-
bien (each under pay at ten shillings sterling per day); Matthew Elliott, Simon Girty, James Girty, George Girty, Pierre
Drouillard, William Tucker, Robert Surplus, Fontenoy Dequindre (each sixteen shillings, York currency, per day); Nicolas
Loraine (ten shillings, York currency); Jeancaire Chabert (eight
shillings, York currency, and ten shillings sterling from 24th
March); Claud Lubute, Henry Baby, Francis Diel, Duplessis,
La Seuexe, Gregor McGregor, Sampson Fleming, Charles Guion,
Thomas McCarty. *24th June*—Francis L'Coellie, D. Dequindre
(each eight shillings, York, per day); John Mackay (four shillings, York). Leith's pay as interpreter would have been the
same as that of Simon Girty, who was thus employed.

[2] The word " exclusively " is here used, as once before by Leith
in this narrative, for " included."

[3] Just what Lieutenant-Governor Hamilton desired of his interpreter is here explicitly given. It was not only " to interpret for
them " (that is, for the Indians then in alliance with Great Britain), but " sometimes to go to war with them against their enemies;" that is, against the frontier settlements of Pennsylvania,
Virginia, and Kentucky. To go to war with them meant, of
course, to take up the hatchet in true Indian style—to kill indis-
criminately men, women, and children.

[4] That is, the Shawanese and Wyandot tongues, else he would

of peculiar service to them. This so affrighted and confused me, that I did not know what answer to give him; but told him, as an excuse, that I was a very unhealthy, weakly youth, and not able to perform such services. He then requested me to go to him the next morning, at nine o'clock; accordingly, I went at that hour. He then enquired if I had considered of the offer he had made me the evening before. I told him I had; and urged the same excuse for not complying with it. He answered,—"If you are not fit for the service, you are not fit for Sandusky; and you will stay where you are." My employer had a partner[1] in the Fort; and I consulted him on the matter. I told him he had better give me a discharge, as the Governor would not let me go. He answered he would not discharge me, but would wait the result of the matter; until which time he would board me at Forsyth's Tavern;[2] and if I got my wages, I need not care where I was. I acquiesced to the proposition, and went there to board. After some time elapsed, while in that situation, as I was sitting in one of the lower rooms, lamenting my condition,

---

not have been engaged to trade at Sandusky, which was a Wyandot town, where the Shawanese also frequently brought their peltry. Leith could also speak the Delaware language; but this tribe had not yet left the Muskingum and Tuscarawas.

[1] One Robbins.

[2] The principal hostelry at that date in Detroit.

lest some sad misfortune should befall me, I heard some men enter the house above; they inquired of the landlady if there was a man by the name of Leeth boarding there. She answered in the affirmative; and they observed, they would be glad to see him. She came down and informed me, that some gentlemen above wished to see me; and requested I would go up. I answered her, that I was afraid their visit portended no good to me, and I was in a peculiar situation, and felt some fears in going up. She informed me, they were very clever gentlemen, and I need not fear to go up: upon which, I went with her into the room. On my arrival in the room, they presented me with a [10] chair— I sat down. They then, with the utmost complaisance and affability, presented me with some wine;[1] my mind being considerably on the alert, and not knowing their

[1] There seems to have been an abundance of wine in Detroit during the Revolution. Not long subsequent to the incident narrated above, the commanding officer at that post was furnished with four casks of Madeira, of 115 gallons each, at forty shillings per gallon, and one cask of red port, of thirty gallons, at thirty shillings. Other gentlemen were frequently supplied with wine by the cask. In striking contrast with this was its scarcity in the Fort Pitt (Pittsburgh) region during that conflict. In a letter from James Marshel, lieutenant of Washington county, Pennsylvania, to Brigadier-General William Irvine, commanding that post and its dependencies, dated May 29, 1782, the writer says: "I have been asked by a Presbyterian minister and some of his people to request you to spare one

intentions towards me, I refused to take any for some
time; but at length, through their friendly persuasions, I consented and took some. After this ceremony was over, they informed me that they had understood the Governor had refused to give me a pass,
and I was then detained, though on wages, against my
will. I answered in the affirmative; when they let
fall a volley of curses on him, and advised me not
to yield to him; but continue in the Fort. " It may
be," said they, "you do not like to board at the
Tavern; if not, and you had rather be at a private
house, preparation shall be made for you to live with
us." Their complaisance won my affections; and I
accepted their offer. They, being traders also, employed me to spy around the town, and when any
Indians brought skins, furs, &c. to market to deal
for them, in their behalf, as I understood the Indian
language, and had a better opportunity of trafficking
in that way, than themselves; for which they gave me
from two to five dollars per day, for ten weeks; during which time, I was confined to the Fort.[1]

One day, while detained in the Fort, I observed

gallon of wine for the use of a sacrament. If it is in your
power to supply them with this article, I make no doubt you
will do it, as it can not be obtained in any other place in this
country." (*Washington-Irvine Correspondence.* Madison, Wis.:
David Atwood, 1882, p. 290).

[1] Leith's meaning here is that he was not allowed to leave Detroit.

some soldiers drawing the cannon out of the Fort,
and placing them on the bank of the River;[1] and
whilst I was ruminating in my mind, what could be
the meaning of this singular manœuvre, a young silver-
smith, with whom I was intimately acquainted, came
and asked me to walk with him, and see them fire the
cannon. I walked with him to the place where they
had carried them. When we arrived there, we found
Governor Hamilton, and several other British officers,
who were standing and sitting around. Immediately
after our arrival at the place, the Indians produced a
large quantity of scalps;[2] the cannon fired, the Indians
raised a shout, and the soldiers waved their hats, with
huzzas and tremendous shrieks, which lasted some
[11] time.[3] This ceremony being ended, the Indians
brought forward a parcel of American prisoners, as a
trophy of their victories; among whom, were eighteen
women and children, poor creatures, dreadfully mangled
and emaciated; with their clothes tattered and torn to

---

[1] The stream spoken of by Leith was, of course, the Detroit
river.

[2] That these were scalps of men, women, and children, torn
from the heads of inoffensive settlers who had fallen victims to
savage cruelty, is certain; and it is equally certain that, for these
scalps, the savages were paid rewards by Hamilton.

[3] This plain, unvarnished statement shows, beyond all question, the hideousness, the cruelty, the savageness with which the
war was carried on by the British from Detroit and its dependencies against the border settlements.

pieces, in such a manner as not to hide their nakedness; their legs bare and streaming with blood; the effects of being torn with thorns, briars and brush.[1]

To see these poor creatures dragged, like sheep to the slaughter, along the British lines, caused my heart to shrink with throbbings, and my hair to rise with rage; and if ever I committed murder in my heart, it was then, for if I had had an opportunity, and been supported with strength, I should certainly have killed the Governor, who seemed to take great delight in the exhibition.[2] My business hurried me from this horrible scene, and I know not what became of those poor wretches, who were the miserable victims of savage power.

Every man in the Fort, capable of bearing arms, was trained twice a week, while I remained there.—I was taken with them one evening on parade, and there

[1] No one can doubt for a moment the truthfulness of this sad recital; but the most horrible part of the picture was hidden from the narrator's view. The frightful tortures at the stake of un-happy prisoners—what words can describe those savage scenes of daily occurrence in the wilderness during the Revolution!

[2] If additional testimony were required to fix upon the memory of Lieutenant-Governor Henry Hamilton the stamp of most bar-barous cruelty, this one declaration of Leith's that " he seemed to take great delight in the exhibition," would suffice; no more, certainly, is needed. To those writers who would fain attempt to mitigate the atrocity of his conduct, the above positive assertion of an eye-witness is commended for their careful consideration.

seemed to be a kind of providence in it, for it was the means of my not being draughted, as, on that day, I was taken with the ague and fever, and was not fit for service. My employers were very kind to me, and paid every attention in their power. On the next morning, between daylight and sunrise, the drums beat to arms, when my two employers rose immediately, dressed themselves, and obeyed the call. I, also, took my rifle and followed. One of them observing me, asked me where I was going. I answered, I supposed I must go on parade with them. They advised me to go back and go to bed, for there would be a general draught that day, and that I would be the first man draughted, if I were found in the ranks. I went back and did as they directed me, and with fears, and awful apprehensions, waited their return. About 10 o'clock, they returned, and said they had told me [12] in the morning I would be the first man called in the draught, which was truly the case, but said they answered to my name, and informed the Governor that I was lying sick at their house; and he made no reply. I remained with them for three weeks more, under partly pretended, and partly real sickness ; at the end of which time, my old employer's partner[1] came to my habitation, and informed me that a favorable opportunity then offered itself for me to leave the Fort, and if I would make

---

[1] Whose name, it will be remembered, was Robbins.

application to the Governor, I might probably get a
pass. I, accordingly, waited on the Governor, and told
him I had remained a considerable time in the Fort, with
my employer's goods, and should be very glad to have
an opportunity of taking them to the place of destination, which I could not do without his signature to a
pass, which would permit me to leave the Fort. He
asked me when I would be ready to start. I told him
if I could obtain his permission, I would be ready to
start the next morning. He then asked me if I would
take some provisions with me. I enquired how much
he wanted taken. He answered, four barrels of flour
and two of pork, which he wanted left on the way. I
answered him, my Boat would be considerably crowded,
but I could take that quantity. On that condition, he
gave me liberty to go, and sent his provisions on board
the Boat the same evening. As I passed the door, going out of his office, the guard observed to me, now
you will have to go to the Chief Justice,[1] and procure
a certificate, before your pass is valid. I then went to

---

[1] Philip Dejain. On the 24th day of April, 1767, Captain
George Trumbull, of the 60th (or Royal American) regiment,
commandant of Detroit and its dependencies, issued a commission to him as justice of the peace and notary. He also received
another commission on the 28th of July following from Robert
Bayard, major, commanding at that post. Dejain was a mer-
chant who had been unfortunate in his business. He spoke both
English and French.

him, and asked him for a certificate, on which he asked me where was my bail. I informed him I had no bail procured, nor did I know there was any needed under such circumstances.—" Well," said he, " you can not go until you furnish bail, neither can I give you a certificate." [1] I then went to my employer's partner, and informed him that matters stood worse with me than ever, for I could not get off without giving bail in the sum of five hundred pounds sterling, which I had no idea I could do, and [13] must still remain in the Fort. He then observed he would go my bail. He went with me to the Chief Justice, entered bail for me, and I obtained a certificate.[1] Having procured the proper documents for my departure, I set sail next morning, with two hands beside myself, and on the third day arrived at Sandusky,[2] where I found my employer in good

---

[1] As will soon be shown, Leith had but little, if any, idea of the conditions of the bond.

[2] In going from Detroit to Lower Sandusky by water, Leith sailed down the Detroit river, across the west end of Lake Erie, into Sandusky bay, and up the bay and Sandusky river to his point of destination—the lower Wyandot town upon that river. This point during the Revolution was the port of entry for supplies for the Wyandots, Shawanese and Mingoes, and, before the close of the war, for the Delawares also. Here, too, British soldiers, officers and employes of the British Indian department, and, as we have seen, British traders, made their first landing on their way to those tribes from Detroit.

health, anxiously waiting my arrival. I continued with
him, and in his employ, until about the middle of October[1] following; when, one morning, he appeared to
have some very serious reflections; and after a deep
study, observed to me, we should have to go to Detroit
in a few days. I informed him, that the situation of
the place was about as it was when I left there, and
I had had such difficulties there before, I believed
I should not go there again, while the place was
in that situation; for it was probable I might again
meet with the same, or worse difficulties. He then observed, I must go, or Robins,[2] his partner, would have

[1] That is, by the middle of October, 1777. It will be presently
seen that Leith, some days after, saw Lieutenant-Governor Henry
Hamilton in Detroit; but that official left there on the 7th of October, 1778, and did not return; so that the October spoken of by
Leith must have been in 1777.

[2] One of the Moravian missionaries, on his way in 1782 from
Upper Sandusky to Detroit, along with other missionaries and
their families, stopped at Lower Sandusky. There he found a
Mr. Arundle and Mr. Robbins, residing as traders. He says:

" Arriving at Lower Sandusky [in March, 1782], after several
days traveling through the wilderness and swampy grounds; we
were kindly received, by two English traders, who resided about
a mile from each other, with the principal village of the Wyandots between them. Mr. Arundle, having a spacious house, took
in those who had families, while Mr. Robbins made the two sin-
gle brethren welcome at his house; our conductor lodged with
the former. With the assistance of Mr. Arundle, a letter was immediately written to the commandant at Detroit [Major A. S. De

to pay the £500, for which he was bail for me, when I left there. I had not known before, that an obligation

Peyster], and sent by express to inform him of our arrival at this place."—Heckewelder's *Narrative*, pp. 329, 330.

From what is here said, and from certain other extrinsic evidence, the conclusion is that Messrs. Arundle and Robbins were partners—the same who employed Leith when he first arrived at Detroit in 1777.

The following recital may not be devoid of interest in this connection:

"In the spring of the year 1782, the war-chief [Abraham Kuhn] of the Wyandots of Lower Sandusky sent a white prisoner (a young man [name unknown], whom he had taken at Fort McIntosh) as a present to another chief, who was called the *Half-King* of Upper Sandusky, for the purpose of being adopted into his family, in the place of one of his sons, who had been killed [in the celebrated Poe fight] the preceding year, while at war with the people on the Ohio. The prisoner arrived, and was presented to the Half-King's wife, but she refused to receive him, which, according to the Indian rule, was, in fact, a sentence of death. The young man was, therefore, taken away for the purpose of being tortured and burnt on the pile. While the dreadful preparations were making near the village, the unhappy victim being already tied to the stake, and the Indians arriving from all quarters to join in the cruel act or to witness it, two English traders, Messrs. *Arundle* and *Robbins* (I delight in making this honorable mention of their names), shocked at the idea of the cruelties which were about to be perpetrated, and moved by feelings of pity and humanity, resolved to unite their exertions to endeavor to save the prisoner's life by offering a ransom to the war-chief [Abraham Kuhn], which he, however refused, because, said

rested on my bail for my return, or, I believe, I should
not have left there under such circumstances. However, I determined to relieve my bail; and the next
morning we started for Detroit. When we arrived there,
I waited on the Governor,[1] with my employer; and gave

he, it was an established rule among them, that when a prisoner
who had been given as a present, was refused adoption, he was
irrevocably doomed to the stake, and it was not in the power of
any one to save his life. Besides, added he, the numerous war
captains who were on the spot, had it in charge to see the sentence
carried into execution. The two generous Englishmen, however, were not discouraged, and determined to try a last effort.
They well knew what effects the high-minded pride of an Indian
was capable of producing, and to this strong and noble passion
they directed their attacks. 'But,' said they, in reply to the answer
which the chief had made them, ' among all those chiefs whom
you have mentioned, there is none who equals you in greatness ;
you are considered not only as the greatest and bravest, but as the
best man in the nation.' ' Do you really believe what you say?'
said at once the Indian, looking them full in the face. ' Indeed,
we do.' Then, without saying another word, he blackened himself, and, taking his knife and tomahawk in his hand, made his way
through the crowd to the unhappy victim, crying out with a loud
voice, ' What have you to do with *my* prisoner?' and at once cut-
ting the cords with which he was tied, took him to his house
which was near Mr. Arundle's, whence he was forthwith secured
and carried off by safe hands to Detroit."—Heckewelder's *Ind.
Nations*, pp. 162. 163.

[1]After the capture of the Illinois country by George Rogers
Clark, Hamilton at Detroit planned an expedition for its recovery,
to be commanded by himself. It proved a failure, and the com-

up my pass and certificate to him. Now, said I to my employer, you need not depend on my services any longer, for I will never again plunge myself into such difficulties, or attempt to get another pass, or give bail in this place ; for I now feel myself a free man, and will go where I please. He told me, I had better take good care in what I said, for if any of the British heard me use such expressions, they would immediately inform against me, and I would be put on board the guard-ship then lying at anchor there.

mander fell into the hands of Clark. Among others captured was his "grand judge," Philip Dejean, before mentioned. Hamilton was sent a prisoner to Virginia, where he, "Grand Judge Dejean," and one Captain La Mothe were, for awhile, ironed and closely imprisoned in a dungeon at Williamsburg ; were prohibited the use of pen, ink and paper, and from all intercourse, by order of the Council of Virginia, who upon examining the evidence before them, found that Hamilton had been guilty of great cruelties to American prisoners at Detroit ; that he had offered rewards for scalps, but none for prisoners, thus inciting the Indians to murder the defenseless ; that Dejean was the willing instrument of his cruelty, and that La Mothe had himself led scalping parties, who spared neither men, women nor children. This imprisonment led to a notable correspondence between Washington and Jefferson, the governer of Virginia, and others, as to whether, as prisoners of war, Hamilton and his companions were not entitled to different treatment. They were subsequently released and paroled. Hamilton was afterwards, for one year, governor of Canada, and was then appointed governor of Dominica, and not long after died.

I continued in the Fort about a week longer;
when, one morning my employer asked me, when I
intended leaving there. I told him, I should go
when I pleas[14]ed. He answered, he wished to know,
because he intended to leave there the next morning;
and if I would meet him at Brownstown,[1] he would
employ an Indian to take my horse around,[2] and take
me on board his boat; "for," said he, "I can not
get along without you."

I concluded I would meet him, and went there the
same evening;[3] where I met him, and got on board
his boat; from whence, we made our way to Sandusky;[4]

---

[1] Brownstown, an Indian village of the Detroit Wyandots,
situated on the site of what is now Gibraltar, a post-village of
Wayne county, Michigan, on the west side of the Detroit river,
at its entrance into Lake Erie, one mile from Gibraltar Station
of the Canada Southern railroad. Adam Brown, a Wyandot
chief, once resided there; hence the name—Brownstown.

[2] That is, around the west end of Lake Erie to Lower
Sandusky.

[3] That Leith was enabled this time to leave Detroit without
giving bail, and his having returned there from Lower Sandusky
without any ostensible reason given by his employer, except
that his partner would have to pay the £500 penalty in his bail-
bond unless he returned, raises a suspicion that the whole matter
was a plan devised by the traders to relieve themselves from the
bond.

[4] It would seem, beyond all doubt, that it was Lower Sandusky, and not Upper Sandusky, to which they made their way
at this time. The location of the former has already been given;

where I remained some time in his employ. Whilst remaining here, a circumstance took place, which was in the utmost degree appalling to human nature; and raised such sensations of horror in my breast, that I never before experienced; and which, the reader may imagine, for I cannot describe them. A prisoner was brought in by the Wyandotts[1] and Mingoes,[2] to the store of my employer. Before the store door were a number of Wyandotts, waiting to join in the murdering of him. As he was passing the house, they knocked him down with tomahawks, cut off his head, and fixed it on a pole, erected for the purpose; when commenced a scene of yelling, dancing, singing and rioting, which, I suppose, represented something like demons from the infernal regions.[3] After their fury and drunken

the last mentioned was about forty miles farther up the Sandusky river.

[1] The valley of the Sandusky, with considerable outlying territory, was then, and had been for many years, the home of Wyandot Indians, who had migrated there from the vicinity of Detroit, where still remained a part of the nation.

[2] The Mingoes had no villages upon the Sandusky river during the revolution; but, to the southward, at not a great distance, there dwelt different bands of these vagrant Iroquois, in a number of villages.

[3] The importance of this recital is, in an historical sense, two-fold. It settles the question: (1.) that the Wyandots were (notwithstanding their professions to the contrary), so early as 1778, actually fighting against the United States as

frolick was abated, we sent to the Chief of the Nation[1]
for liberty to bury the body; and his answer was,
"They do not bury our dead when they kill them,
and we will not bury theirs:" on the return of which,
we sent another petition, and informed him, that we
would remove our store out of the country, if we could
not have liberty to bury dead carcases out of our sight.
He answered then, that we might do as we pleased
with them: on which, we took the head down, placed
it to the body, as well as we could, wrapped them in a
clean blanket, and buried him as decently as our situation would admit of.[2]

---

allies of Great Britain; and (2.) that captives were brought
from the border to points contiguous to Detroit, and then tomahawked and scalped, the direct result of Hamilton's barbarous
policy of offering a reward for scalps, but paying none for
prisoners.

[1] The Chief of the Sandusky Wyandots at this time was the
Half King—so called by the English,—a shrewd but rapacious
savage. His residence was not at Lower Sandusky, but at
Upper Sandusky, then located on the east side of the river,
above what is now a town of the same name, the county-seat of
Wyandot county, Ohio, but afterward moved to the west side
of that stream, about eight miles below its former site, as will
hereafter be explained.

[2] This burial is the *first* one of any white person known to
have taken place within the limits of what is now Sandusky
county, Ohio; and, as first things are, to local historians, important events, it is suggested that this fact may be of interest to future
annalists of that county

⌐Some time after this scene, the Delaware Indian,[1] who first took me, came to Sandusky, on purpose for me, and said, I must go with him. I parleyed with him for some time, and told him I was not ready, and [15] could not leave my business; but through his insinuating persuasions, he, at length, prevailed on me to go. I made ready as soon as possible, and accompanied him to Coshocton, (the Muskingum River,)[2] where I remained a considerable time. ⌐

The Spring following,[3] I was married to a young

---

[1] It may be thought strange that a Delaware, at this period, should be found at Lower Sandusky, as his nation was, if not the ally of the United States, quite friendly. But this state of affairs was peculiar to the nation *at large.* Some bands were, even then, hostile; and it was not long before a considerable number, withdrew from the Muskingum, and made their homes nearer the British allies—the Shawanese, Mingoes, and Wyandots.

[2] Coshocton was then the principal Delaware village, the site, as already explained, of the present town of that name, county-seat of Coshocton county, Ohio. The Muskingum river is formed by the Walhonding and Tuscarawas rivers, which unite at Coshocton. It runs southward, through the present county of Muskingum; southeastward. through the counties of Morgan and Washington, and enters the Ohio river at Marietta. It is about one hundred and twenty miles long. The chief towns upon its banks are Zanesville and Marietta.

[3] That is, " the spring following " the year of Leith's arrival at Coshocton; or, in other words. " the spring of 1779."

woman,[1] seventeen or eighteen years of age; also a prisoner to the Indians; who had been taken by them when
about twenty months old.[2]

I was then in my twenty-fourth year.[3] Our place of
residence was in Moravian Town,[4] for about two years;[5]
about which time, Col. Williams, an American officer,

[1] From the descendants of Leith, I learn that this young
woman's name was Sally Lowrey.

[2] It seems to be certain that Sally Lowrey was taken in 1763,
during what is known in history as Pontiac's war. It is a tra-
dition of the family descendants that she was captured at Big
Cove, in Pennsylania.

[3] As Leith would be very apt to bear in mind his age at his
marriage, this assertion may be considered a verity. Now, as he
was born on the 15th of March, 1755, he would be, in 1779, in his
twenty-fourth year down to the 15th of that month. He must
have been married, therefore, in the first half of March, 1779, as
his nuptials took place in the spring. I know of no marriage
between two white persons of so early a date as this within the
present limits of Ohio.

[4] This town was known as Gnadenhütten. It was a Moravian
missionary town, where were gathered a number of Indians, principally Delawares. It was situated on what was then known as
the Muskingum, now Tuscarawas, in the present Clay township,
Tuscarawas county, Ohio, lying in the outskirts of what is now
the town of the same name.

[5] The idea is, that the two went to live at Gnadenhütten *soon
after their marriage;* this is evident from what follows.

took possession of Coshocton;[1] and shortly after,[2] the

[1] Leith meant Colonel David Williamson; but, in this, he was mistaken. The American officer who "took possession of Coshocton" was Colonel Daniel Brodhead. This was a little over two years after Leith's marriage. Colonel Brodhead, who was then commanding Fort Pitt (Pittsburgh) and its dependencies, left that post on the 7th of April, 1781, with over one hundred and fifty regulars, on an expedition against those Delawares who had become hostile, dropping down to Wheeling, where David Shepherd, lieutenant of Ohio county, Virginia, had collected one hundred and thirty-four of the militia of his county, including officers. With them went a few friendly Indians—Captains Montour and Wilson, and three other warriors—who evinced a keen desire for the scalps of the hostile Delawares. On the 10th, the united force made its way across the Ohio, taking the nearest route to Coshocton. Shepherd's division consisted of four companies. The savages were completely surprised. Their town was laid waste; also a village of theirs just below. Fifteen of their warriors were killed, and over twenty prisoners taken. Large quantities of peltry and other stores were destroyed, and about forty head of cattle killed. The Americans then proceeded up the valley to Newcomer's Town, where there were about thirty friendly Delaware Indians, who were occupying the place. From them, as well as from the Moravian missionaries and their converts, whose towns were not far away, the troops experienced great kindness, obtaining a sufficient supply of meat and corn to subsist themselves and their horses to the Ohio. The expedition proved a decided success; for the hostile Delawares now entirely forsook the valley of the Tuscarawas and Muskingum, never again occupying either as a permanent abode—drawing back to the Scioto, the Mad river, and the Sandusky.

[2] In September following; that is, in September, 1781.

British, and their Indian allies, took Moravian Town,[1] with me, my wife and children,[2] and all the Moravians, prisoners; and carried us to Sandusky.[3] After arriving at Sandusky, the British would not suffer me to trade on my own footing, and for myself:—but five of them having placed their funds into one general stock, employed me to attend to their business for them ; and, two of them being my old employers, they gave me

[1] The town "taken" was Gnadenhütten. The Indians who captured the missionaries and their flock was a party of Delawares, Wyandots, Monseys, and a small number of Shawanese, headed by Matthew Elliott and a few English and French. The reason for the sacking of this missionary Indian town, as given by Moravian writers, is wholly erroneous. The cause was this: the Indians and the British, who were on an expedition against the border, made this village a resting-place ; and, while there, obtained information from prisoners which proved conclusively that the Moravian missionaries had informed the Americans of their intended raid. (See *Washington-Irvine Correspondence*, pp. 58-60.)

[2] The family of Leith consisted of his wife and two children. The eldest, Samuel, died in Fairfield county, Ohio, in 1820. Both his children were boys, and both were born at Gnadenhütten. Samuel having been born in 1780, was the second white child, in point of time, born in the Tuscarawas valley, so far as is now known: the first was John Lewis Roth, born in Gnadenhütten, July 4, 1773.)

[3] The point where the Moravian missionaries and their flock spent the winter of 1782, was on the east bank of the Sandusky river, something over two miles above what is now Upper Sandusky, Wyandot county, Ohio.

the same wages as heretofore. Whilst in this employ, Col's Williams[1] and Crawford[2] marched with an
army, against Sandusky;[3] at which time I was closely

---

[1] Colonel David Williamson. He was Colonel of the Third
Battalion of Washington county militia, and second in command
upon the Sandusky expedition. He was a son of John Williamson, and was born in 1752, near Carlisle, Pennsylvania. He came
to the western country when a boy; he afterward returned home,
and persuaded his parents to emigrate beyond the Alleghanies,
They settled upon Buffalo creek, in what was subsequently Washington county, about twelve miles from the Ohio. At that point,
David had a "station" during the Revolution, which, though
often alarmed, was never attacked. From the commencement
of Indian depredations, Williamson took an active part in the
defense of the western border, having previously, during Dunmore's war, held a captain's commission. He was every-where
recognized as a true lover of his country—willing to make any
sacrifice for its welfare. His activity in guarding the defenseless
inhabitants of the frontier settlements was untiring. His having led
an expedition, early in 1782, to the Tuscarawas, which resulted in
the killing of a large number of Moravian Indians, resulted in his
being severely criticised. After the return of the Sandusky expedition, an account of which is presently given, he was soon
actively engaged in watching the exposed border—continuing his
services until the restoration of peace. He was afterward popular
with the people of his county, being first county lieutenant, and
then elected, in 1787, to the office of sheriff.

[2] Colonel William Crawford, a biographical sketch of whom
is hereafter given. (Page 51, NOTE.)

[3] That is, against Upper Sandusky—a Wyandot Indian village,
situated less than three miles up the Sandusky river, from the site

watched by the Indians; and had to make my movements with particular regularity; though I had spies
going to and fro, by whom, I could hear, every evening, where the army was encamped, for several days.
One evening, I was informed, the army was only
fifteen miles distant;[1] when I immediately sent the
hands to gather the horses, &c. to take our goods to
Lower Sandusky. I packed up the goods, (about
£1500 worth in silver,[2] furs, powder, lead, &c.) with
such agility, that by the next morning, at daylight,
we started for Lower Sandusky. I also took all the
cattle belonging to the company, along. After travelling about three miles, I met Capt. Elliot, a British
officer;[3] and about twelve miles farther on, I met

of the present Upper Sandusky, county-seat of Wyandot county,
Ohio, but on the opposite side of the stream. The village had,
however, been deserted some time before; and its occupants had
moved some distance down the river on the west side, at a point
five miles below the site of what is now Upper Sandusky. Its
locality was in the present Crane township, Wyandot county,
Ohio, just where what is now known as the "Kilbourne road"
crosses the Sandusky river. It was here that Leith was living
with his family when the Sandusky was approached by Crawford and his army.

[1] At a point not far from the present village of Wyandot,
Wyandot, county, Ohio.

[2] By "silver" is meant silver ornaments, such as were worn
by the Indians.

[3] Matthew Elliott was an Irishman by birth. He had for-

the whole British army, composed of Col. Butler's
Rangers.[1] They took from me [16] my cattle, and
let me pass. That night I encamped about fourteen
miles above Lower Sandusky; when, just after I had

merly resided in Pennsylvania, east of the Alleghany Mountains, and early engaged in the Indian trade, headquarters at
Fort Pitt. He was thus employed when hostilities began, in
1774, between the Virginians and the Mingoes and Shawanese.
He remained in the Indian country until after the battle of Point
Pleasant and the marching of Lord Dunmore to the Scioto
river, protected by the savages. He was, in fact, their messenger, sent by the Shawanese asking terms of peace with the
Virginia governor. After the ending of "Lord Dunmore's
war," he again traded from Fort Pitt, with the Indians beyond
the Ohio, continuing until about the middle of November, 1776,
when he was captured near what is now Dresden, Muskingum
county, Ohio, by a party of six Wyandots, his goods confiscated,
and himself and assistant, one Michael Herbert, taken to Detroit. The next year he was released on parole, and returned
to Pittsburgh by way of Quebec. In April, 1778, along with
Alexander McKee and Simon Girty, he fled his country, and
hastening into the wilderness, finally reached Detroit, where he
was welcomed as a loyalist by the British, and engaged by
Governor Hamilton in the British Indian department. When
met by Leith he was making his way in all haste from Lower
Sandusky to the assistance of the Wyandots and their allies
against Crawford.

[1] The "whole British army, composed of Colonel Butler's
Rangers," was a body of British soldiers under command of
Captain William Caldwell, who, like Captain Elliott, was
hastening to the aid of the Indians at Upper Sandusky.

encamped, and put out my horses to graze, there came to my camp, a man, who was a French interpreter to the Indians.[1] "Well," said he, "I believe I will stay with you, to-night, and take care of you." I told him, he could remain there for the night; but I intended starting early in the morning. Next morning, after we had got our horses loaded, ready to start, and the Frenchman had mounted his horse, we heard a cannon fire at Upper Sandusky.[2] The Frenchman clapped his hand to his breast, and said, "I shall be there before the battle is begun:" but, alas, poor fellow! he got there too soon: without fear, or any thought but victory, he went on to where a parcel of Indians were painting and preparing for battle, put on a ruffled shirt, and painted a red spot on his breast; saying, "Here is a mark for the Virginia riflemen;" and shortly after, marched with the Indians to battle; where, in a short time, he received a ball in the very spot, and died instantaneously.[3] I arrived at Lower Sandusky, on the second day, and remained there three

[1] Francis Le Villier. (See *Washington-Irvine Correspondence*, pp. 305, 368.)

[2] Captain Caldwell had cannon with him; but Leith was mistaken in supposing that the firing was at Upper Sandusky. The party having them in charge had not yet reached that point.

[3] The fact of Le Villier's death is corroborated by the official report of Captain Caldwell, written at Lower Sandusky, June 11, 1782.

days to hear the event. At length, the Americans under Col. Williams,[1] stole a retreat on the Indians, who were gathering around them in great numbers ; but Col. Crawford, with the most of his men, were taken by them.[2] They tomahawked all his men, and burnt him

[1] The name here given by Leith was intended for "William-son," as in a previous instance.

[2] Of the volunteers who went upon the expedition against San-dusky, about two-thirds were from Washington county, Pennsyl-vania ; the residue, except a few from Ohio county, Virginia, were from Westmoreland. The final rendezvous was at the Mingo bottom on the west side of the Ohio river, where, on the twenty-fourth day of May, 1782, four hundred and eighty, finally, con-gregated. They distributed themselves into eighteen companies. The general officers elected were : for colonel - commandant, Colonel Wm. Crawford ; for four field majors (to rank in the or-der named), David Williamson, Thomas Gaddis, John McClel-land, and James Brenton ; for brigade major, Daniel Leet. Dr. John Knight went as surgeon ; John Rose, as aid. The guides were Thomas Nicholson, John Slover and Jonathan Zane.

The volunteers began their march the next day for Upper San-dusky. All were mounted. On the fourth of June, the enemy were encountered a short distance north of what is now Upper Sandusky, Ohio. They numbered something over three hundred, consisting of about two hundred savages—Wyandots, Delawares, Mingoes, and "Lake Indians"—beside the company of rangers from Detroit, under command of Captain William Caldwell. A battle ensued, with the advantage on the side of the Americans. The loss of the enemy was five killed—four Indians and a ran-ger—and eleven wounded, including Captain Caldwell ; the

alive.   After the decisive battle, my employers again in-

American loss was five killed and nineteen wounded.   The next
day (June 5th) the enemy were re-enforced by not less than one
hundred and forty Shawanese and by a small detachment of rangers.   Crawford called a council of war, and it was decided to
retreat.

The return march began soon after dark of the same day, but
was attended with considerable confusion.   The main portion of
the retreating army was joined the next morning by some strag-
gling parties, so that the whole numbered about three hundred ;
and the retreat was continued.   Quite a number were missing ;
among them were Colonel Crawford, Dr. Knight, Major McClel-
land and John Slover.   In the afternoon (June 6th), the volunteers were overtaken by a force of the enemy, in what is now
Crawford county, Ohio, and a warm engagement ensued ; but the
pursuers were driven off, with a loss to the Americans of three
killed and eight wounded.   The expedition finally reached the
Mingo bottom on their return ; and recrossed the Ohio on the
thirteenth of June, having with them a number of their wounded.
The next day the army disbanded.   The entire loss was about
fifty men.   Of those taken by the enemy, only two escaped—Dr.
Knight and John Slover.   A number of the captured were tomahawked ; but Colonel Crawford, his son-in-law (Wm. Harrison),
and a few others (all of whom had been made prisoners), were
tortured at the stake.   Crawford perished miserably, amidst the
most terrible suffering, on the eleventh of June, in what is now
Wyandot county, Ohio.   (For an extended narrative of this campaign, see *An Historical Account of the Expedition against
Sandusky, under Colonel William Crawford, in* 1782. *With
Biographical Sketches, Personal Reminiscences, and Descrip-
tions of Interesting Localities; Including, also, Details of the*

sisted on my moving the store to Upper Sandusky, which

Disastrous Retreat, the Barbarities of the Savages, and the Awful Death of Crawford by Torture. Cincinnati: Robert Clarke & Co., 1873.)

NOTE.—William Crawford was born in Westmoreland county, Virginia; his family, however, early moved to Frederick county, beyond the Blue Ridge. Here he married Hannah Vance. He was about ten years older than Washington, but was taught by the latter the art of surveying. Up until the commencement of the old French war, Crawford's principal duties were such as usually appertain to a farmer's life. In 1755, he forsook the compass and the plow for

"The pomp and circumstance of glorious war,"

receiving from the governor of Virginia a commission as ensign. He was first employed in garrison duty, or as a scout upon the frontiers. In 1758, he marched with the Virginia troops, under Washington, to Fort Duquesne, which post was reached and occupied in November. Crawford remained in the service, being promoted first to a lieutenantcy — afterwards commissioned as captain. At the close of hostilities, he returned to his home and resumed his labors of farmer and surveyor. In Pontiac's war, which followed the seven years' war, he took an active part, doing efficient service in protecting the frontiers from savage incursions.

While in the Virginia army, Crawford became familiar with the country watered by the Monongahela and its branches. He had, indeed, become enamored of the trans-Alleghany region, and resolved, at some future day, to make it his home. The time had now arrived to put his resolution into practical effect. Early, therefore, in the summer of 1765, he reached the Youghiogheny river, where, at a place then known as "Stewart's Crossings,"

I did as soon as practicable; where I remained about

in what is now Fayette county, Pennsylvania, he chose his future residence; moving his family, consisting of his wife and three children, over the mountains in the spring of 1766. With Crawford, at this place, the next year, Washington opened a correspondence, which continued until near the time of the above letter. (See *The Washington-Crawford Letters.* Cincinnati: Robert Clarke & Co., 1877.)

Among the first employments of Crawford after his removal, besides farming, were surveying and trading with the Indians. During the year 1770, he was appointed one of the justices of the peace for his county, Cumberland, then the most westerly county of Pennsylvania. In the autumn of that year, he received a visit, at his humble cabin upon the Youghiogheny, from Washington, who was then on a tour down the Ohio. Crawford accompanied his friend to the Great Kanawha, the party returning to "Stewart's Crossings" late in November, whence Washington leisurely made his way back to Mt. Vernon.

In March, 1771, Bedford county having been formed from that part of Cumberland including the home of Crawford, he was appointed by Governor Penn one of the justices of the peace for the new county; and in 1773, the erection of Westmoreland from Bedford taking in his residence, he was commissioned one of the "justices of the court of general quarter sessions of the peace, and of the county court of common pleas" for that county. As he was first named on the list of justices, he became by courtesy and usage the president judge of Westmoreland—the first to hold that office in the county. He was, the same year, appointed surveyor for the Ohio company by the college of William and Mary.

In 1773, Lord Dunmore, the Governor of Virginia, paid a visit to Crawford, at his house upon the Youghiogheny, the occasion

three years in their employment.[1] About that time

being turned to profitable account by both parties—by the Earl, in getting reliable information of desirable lands; by Crawford, in obtaining promises for patents for such as he had sought out and surveyed. The next year (1774) occurred "Lord Dunmore's war," a conflict between the Virginians on the one side, and the Shawanese and Mingoes, principally, on the other. In this contest, Crawford was a prominent actor;—first as captain of a company on a scouting expedition, building, subsequently, along with Major Angus McDonald, a fort at the present site of Wheeling; afterward as major in command of troops belonging to the division of the army which descended the Ohio to the mouth of Hocking river, in what is now the State of Ohio. The only fighting done in the Indian country after the bloody battle of Point Pleasant, on the 10th of October, was by a detachment under Crawford, in what is now Franklin county, Ohio, where he surprised and destroyed two Mingo villages, securing some prisoners, as well as considerable amount of plunder, and rescuing two white captives.

The interest taken by Crawford in this war operated greatly to uprejdice his Pennsylvania friends against him; for, among them, the conflict had been an exceedingly unpopular one. Crawford, who, at first, had sided with Pennsylvania in the boundary controversy subsisting between it and Virginia, now took part with the latter; so he was ousted from all offices held by him under authority of the former province. In December, 1774, he had been commissioned by Dunmore a justice of the peace and a justice of oyer and terminer for the county of

---

[1] From what follows in his narrative, it will be noticed that Leith's remembrance as to the time was a little at fault; it was about two years and a half.

they dissolved partnership; when each man took his

Augusta, the court to be held at Fort Dunmore (Pittsburgh). He did not qualify, however, for these offices until after he had been superseded in those held by him under Pennsylvania authority. Augusta county, as claimed by Virginia, included Crawford's home upon the Youghiogheny; afterward the district of West Augusta was formed out of that county. Crawford's place of residence then fell in that district. Finally, when Yohogania county was established, his cabin came within its boundaries, and so remained until Virginia relinquished her claim to south-western Pennsylvania.

Crawford not only took office under Virginia, but he became an active partisan in extending the jurisdiction of his native province over the disputed territory. Some of his acts were doubtless oppressive, though he soon atoned for them in his patriotic course upon the breaking out of the Revolution. The partisan feeling in his breast immediately gave place to the noble one of patriotism. He struck hands with Pennsylvanians in the cause of liberty.

In 1776 Crawford entered the revolutionary service as Lieu-tenant-Colonel of the Fifth Virginia Regiment—William Peachy, colonel. He remained with his regiment until called to the command of the Seventh, in place of William Dangerfield, re-signed. Afterwards, being assigned to the duty of raising a new regiment—the Thirteenth Virginia—he resigned his command of the Seventh. His time thus far had been spent east of the mountains; but now, late in the year, he returned to his home, as the Thirteenth—"West Augusta regiment"—was to be raised west of the Alleghanies. In August, 1777, with about two hun-dred of his new levies, Crawford joined the main army under Washington, who was then near Philadelphia. He rendered

own share of the goods, &c. and entered into business

efficient service in the preliminary movements which resulted in the battle of Brandywine, and in that contest not only took an active and prominent part, but came near being captured. He was also, it seems, in the battle of Germantown. Just before this, General Joseph Reed wrote Washington that he had "Colonel Crawford" with him, "a very good officer."

Late in 1777 Crawford returned to his home, having been sent to the West by Washington to take a command under Brigadier-General Edward Hand. The Commander-in-Chief, in writing to the Board of War, on the 23d of the following May, spoke of Crawford as "a brave and active officer." His being ordered to the Western Department lost him the command of the Thirteenth Virginia and his place in the continental line, which Washington, although he regretted the circumstance, could not get restored to him. Under Brigadier-General Lachlan McIntosh, who succeeded Hand in August, 1778, at Pittsburgh, Crawford took command of the militia of the western counties of Virginia, and had in charge the building of Fort McIntosh at what is now Beaver, in Beaver county, Pennsylvania. He marched with that officer into the Indian country in November, in command of a brigade, and was present at the building, in December, of Fort Laurens, upon the west bank of the Tuscarawas river, in what is now Tuscarawas county, Ohio. He returned soon after to his home, and, in the spring, again marched under McIntosh into the wilderness to the relief of that post. Crawford had now but few prospects before him in a military way, nevertheless he lost no opportunity, when called upon, in serving his country, for he still held his commission as colonel, and continued to hold it until his death.

Notwithstanding the time spent by him in the army, Crawford found leisure to fill several positions of honor and trust to which

for himself. One of them informed me, he was going
to establish a store at New Coshocton,[1] on the head
waters of the Miami River;[2] and if I would go with
him, he would give me the same wages as heretofore;
upon which, I agreed, and went with him.

---

he had been called by his fellow-citizens at home. In November, 1776, he was appointed Deputy Surveyor of Yohogania
county, and sat at intervals in 1777 and the following year as one
of its judges. In 1778 he was one of the commissioners for
adjusting and settling the boundary line between Yohogania and
Ohio counties, Virginia; and, in 1779, was commissioned as
surveyor of his county, continuing in that office to the time of
his death, which occurred before the return of the expedition
against the Wyandots upon the Sandusky, as related in the
previous note.

[1] New Coshocton, a Delaware town, was three miles north
of the site of the present Bellefontaine, Logan county, Ohio.
It was also known as Buckongehelas' (or Pokongekalas') town.
Leith took his wife and two children with him. He had not a
great distance to travel; about forty-five miles in a southwest
direction. The town was on a creek flowing southwest into the
Great Miami, in what is now Miami township, Logan county,
Ohio.

[2] Miami (or Great Miami) river rises in Hardin county,
Ohio, and drains part of Logan county. It runs southwestward
through Shelby county and southward through Miami county to
Dayton, below which it flows southwestward, intersecting the
counties of Butler and Hamilton, and entering the Ohio river
at the southwest extremity of the state, about three miles above
Lawrenceburg, Indiana.

[17] Sometime in the following Fall, the treaty between the Americans and Indians, took place at Fort
Pitt; when I went with the Indians to the treaty,[1] and
left my wife and children behind, at New Coshocton.[2]
After matters were settled, and articles of peace signed,

---

[1] The treaty here referred to was that of Fort McIntosh, held
in January, 1785; but the Indians who were present came in
December, 1784, which was also the month of Leith's arrival.
Fort McIntosh was located near what is now the borough of
Beaver, Beaver county, Pennsylvania, on the north side of the
Ohio river, about thirty miles down that stream from Pittsburgh.

[2] "A grand council was held some little time ago at Coshocking, on the head waters of the Big Miami, at which were the
chiefs of many nations." (Statement of Alex. McCormick to
Captain Doughty, October, 1785, in *The St. Clair Papers*, Vol.
II., p. 10, note.) Coshocking is a well-known synonymn for
Coshocton. As the town was first occupied during the Revolution, Leith speaks of it as New Coshocton. Its locality has
already been pointed out.

"I proceeded up the Miami [in the latter part of March,
1786], which I found very rapid; and on the 27th of April I fell
in with a Delaware town [New Coshocton, as called by Leith],
the residence of Pokonge-Kalas, a chief of great repute. I left
this town on the 10th of May, on my way to Sandusky, having
been, from the 27th of April, at two Shawanese and four Delaware
towns, and some scattering settlements of Wyandots. On the
12th of May, I arrived at the Delaware and Wyandot towns at
Sandusky, where I stayed three days—left it on the 15th, and
arrived at [Fort] McIntosh on the 28th of May." (Liebert's
Report, July 20, 1786, in *The St. Clair Papers*, Vol. II., pp. 16
and 17, note).

I joined in partnership with two others,[1] in a trading association; and in a short time, started westward, with thirty-four horses, loaded with £1484 worth of goods. I went to Tuscarawas,[2] and stayed about nine months; in which time, I had sold out nearly all our goods. About three months after I arrived there, Capt. Hamilton, an American officer,[3] came there with another store, and set up close by me; about which time, I got

[1] One of whom was Mr. David Duncan, of Pittsburgh; the other's name was Wilson.

[2] This was the old Tuscarawas town, situated on the south side of the Tuscarawas river. It was a little below the old Indian ford, but above the forks; that is, above the mouth of Sandy creek. It was known as "Beaver Town at Tuscarawas" in 1764. It was not far from what is now the site of Bolivar, Tuscarawas county, Ohio.

Tuscarawas river drains a part of Summit county, Ohio, and runs southward through Stark and Tuscarawas counties. It finally flows westward, and unites with the Mohican (or Walhonding, sometimes called the White Woman) at Coshocton, in Coshocton county, to form the Muskingum. It is about one hundred and twenty-five miles long. The chief town upon this stream is Massillon, Stark county.

[3] The American army, at this date, was what was called the "First American Regiment." It was under the command of Lieutenant-Colonel Josiah Harmar, headquarters at Fort McIntosh. There was no captain in his force of the name of Hamilton; it is probable, therefore, the captain spoken of by Leith *had been* "an American officer," but was not one at that time. Hamilton had a partner by the name of Greenough, as will be presently seen.

my wife and children with me again.[1] Some time after, while Capt. Hamilton was gone to Fort Pitt, after goods, several Wyandott Indians came to his store; two of them killed his clerk,[2] and bore off all his goods; at which, I was sorely frightened and alarmed, lest they should next serve me in the same way.

While I was sadly ruminating on what might befall me, a Delaware Indian, (one of my old acquaintances,) came to me, and said, "John, I will stand by you, and if you die, I will die by you." We went out soon after, and saw the poor fellow's body lying naked on the ground; we immediately prepared, and started from that place, leaving the naked body of Hamilton's clerk, lying on the ground. On my journey, I fully determined to kill the Indian who had tomahawked him; and thought, when we got to a thicket on Sugar-creek[3] bottom, I would accomplish it; but before we arrived there, I got an opportunity to speak to my wife; when, I told her, my design was to kill that Indian,

[1] He had left them, it will be remembered, at New Coshocton.

[2] James Chambers.

[3] Sugar creek rises in what is now Wayne county, Ohio, runs southeastward, intersects the present Stark county, and enters the Tuscarawas river at what is now Canal Dover, Tuscarawas county, Ohio. The stream is about fifty miles in length. From the Tuscarawas town to the Shawanese villages upon the Mad river, a branch of the Big Miami, Leith and his family had to cross Sugar creek; as it was to these towns, as will presently be seen, that Leith and his family were taken.

and make my escape. She immediateiy burst into tears, and said, "O, John! would you use me so? to kill him, and make your escape, leaving me and my helpless children to the unabating fury of savage barbarity."[1] This so affected me, that I determined to stay and suffer with her, while I lived, let what [18] might, turn up. Three days before this event took place, I dreamed that my head was cut off, and a new one put on, and tied with a silk handkerchief:—after my new head was put on, I thought I would bury my old one, and dug a hole under the sill of the storehouse; but when I got the hole dug, I thought something would hurt my head, and refrained. I made two more attempts to bury it; though it appeared as if I could see the ashes blow in my eyes.

We were then taken to the Shawnee Towns on Mad River;[2] and while I was there, the Indians hid all

---

[1] Here, again, Leith's editor has probably indulged in a slight rhetorical flourish.

[2] Mad river rises in Logan county, Ohio, and runs southward through Champlain county to near Springfield, in Clark county. Below this, it runs southwestward, touching the noithwest part of Greene county, and enters the Miami river at Dayton, Ohio. Its length is about one hundred miles. The Shawanese towns were: A small village called Wapakoneta, on a small creek emptying into Mad river, in what is now Salem township, Champaign county, Ohio, about two and a half miles south of the present town of West Liberty, in Logan county; a village called Mac-a-chack (now usually written and pronounced Mac-a-cheek)

my property at Tuscarawas. After some time, I got
a man to go with me to Fort Pitt;[1] where I pur-

on a creek of the same name, on the north side of the stream,
something over a mile northeast of the site of West Liberty; a
village known as Pigeon town, on the west side of Mad river,
about three miles northwest of Mac-a-check; a town named
Wapatomica, just below the present town of Zanesville; and
another village, on the site of what is now Bellefontaine, called
Blue Jacket's town—all in the present county of Logan, Ohio.

[1] Leith reached Fort McIntosh, on his way to Fort Pitt, about
the middle of October, 1785. Here Major John Doughty was in
command under Lieutenant-Colonel Josiah Harmar. Fortunately
enough, Major Doughty took the sworn statement of Leith concerning the Tuscarawas affair and what followed immediately
thereafter. Leith's affidavit (for which I am indebted to that ex-
cellent work, *The St. Clair Papers*, by Hon. William Henry
Smith, Vol. II, pp. 632, 633,) was as follows:

"The deponent saith that he was storekeeper for himself and
company at Tuscarawas, where he had a quantity of goods and
furs; that there was another store at the same place, kept by
James Chambers, for Messrs. Hamilton and Greenough, where
was also a considerable amount of goods and skins; that the
whole property in both stores was about the value of one thousand
pound [sterling].

"That on Tuesday, the 27th of September [1785], seven of the
Wyandot nation came to the store, about nine o'clock in the morning; the deponent and Chambers were together at his house, sitting by the fire; the Wyandots told the Delawares, a party of
whom had been trading with him [Leith] for some days, that
there was war—that the hatchet was taken up; upon which, one
of the Delawares came to him [Leith] and bid him rise and go

chased horses to go in search of my goods. The

with him; the deponent went with him, when the Delaware told
him that Chambers would be killed; he [Leith] soon heard the
stroke made at Chambers by one of the Wyandots; he [Cham-
bers] was immediately tomahawked and drawn out before the
house, where he was left; the deponent having been a prisoner
with the Delawares for twelve years, and being adopted as a
brother in that nation, was the reason, he supposes, why his life
was spared; the Wyandots took the goods and furs, except the
property of the deponent, and made two parcels of them; they
gave one division to the Delawares and took the other themselves.

"The deponent was carried to the Delaware towns to a place
called Coshurking [New Coshocton], on the head waters of the
Big Miami; at the time of his arrival, there was a grand council
of the Indians, at which were present the chiefs of the Delawares,
Wyandots, Shawanese, Mingoes, Cherokees, Pottawattamies,
Kickapoos, and the Twightwees [Miamis], with belts and speeches
from the Ouiatenons, Tawas [Ottawas], Chippewas, and the Fox
nation. The council was held on the first of October, and lasted
two days and nights; they held it three miles from the town; he
[Leith] could not learn the object of their meeting.

"The deponent further saith that he met with Captain Pipe at
the council, and as soon as the council was over, the deponent
was released from confinement; Captain Pipe and George Washington [an Indian] went with him to Pipe's residence, a Delaware
town on the Sandusky river [rather, on the Tymochtee, a branch
of the Sandusky, in what is now Wyandot county, Ohio]; they
immediately went to work to collect the goods that were taken at
Tuscarawas, and had collected a considerable quantity to be re-
delivered to the owners; they staid two nights at Pipe's town,
when Pipe, George Washington and the deponent went to the
Wyandot towns [on the Sandusky, not far away], where they

third day we arrived at Tuscarawas; and after a considerable search, found them all. I carried them to

were collecting the goods also; that the chiefs of both nations
seemed very averse to the outrage committed at Tuscarawas;
the deponent verily believes that a considerable quantity of the
goods will be returned; the deponent is of the opinion from the
frequent conversations he has had with the Indians, before and
since the late affair at Tuscarawas, that the chiefs of the Delaware and Wyandot nations are for peace, but that the young men
and bad characters of both nations can not be kept at peace; that
Simon Girty [a renegade American] and Captain [William]
Caldwell, of the British rangers, were lately at the Wyandot
towns, and that he verily believes, from the information given
him by a man well acquainted with these matters, that Girty and
Caldwell were using their endeavors to prevent the Delawares
and Wyandots from going to the treaty to be held at the mouth
of the Big Miami [which treaty was then being advocated by the
United States to be holden with the Indians].

"The deponent further saith that from every observation he
could make, and from the general talk of the Indians, he is led
to believe that they are, in general, averse to giving up their
lands; he is certain it will be dangerous for the Continental sur-
veyors to go on with their business, until some further treaty is
made with the Shawanese, Mingoes, and Cherokees, who appear
to be most averse to this business.

"The deponent further saith that he was at the Lower Sandusky
[now Fremont, Sandusky county, Ohio,] when the articles of
peace between Great Britain and America were made known to
the Indians; that they were told that the hatchet was only laid
down, but not buried; that the Half-King [head chief] of the
Wyandots remarked that if it was peace, it should be buried—

Fort Pitt, and returned to my family :[1] after staying
with them some time, I again went to Fort Pitt, with
the intention of dissolving partnership. I informed
my partners, that the times were very dangerous, and
trade very uncertain; and if they were willing, we would
dissolve, and quit business; at any rate for the present:
but they had just purchased a large assortment of
goods; and told me, if I would venture my body,
they would the goods. I then agreed to set out once
more.

I left Fort Pitt about the 15th of January ;[2] and
fixed up a store, in the woods, at Coshocton, at the
mouth of Whitewoman creek.[3] In a short time, I collected about fourteen horse-loads of skins and furs.
The hand[4] I had with me, set out with them, for Fort
Pitt; and after getting about two-thirds of the way,

that there were many of their foolish young men who would take
it up, unless it was covered. And further saith not.

"Sworn to before me, at Fort McIntosh, this 17th day of
October, 1785.   JOHN DOUGHTY,
                                          "Major Comm'dt."

[1] Then at New Coshocton, it will be remembered.

[2] This was in the year 1786.

[3] This stream is still known as the White Woman, but usually
designated as the Mohican, or Walhonding. It is formed by the
Black Fork and Clear Fork, which unite in the south part of
what is now Ashland county, Ohio.

[4] It is a matter of regret that the name of this man is not
given by Leith.

the Mingo and Wyandot Indians overtook him, killed him, and took the horses, and all the loading, off with them. I continued there with my family,[1] and several horses, until about the first of April, under great apprehensions and fears. I then moved to Tapacon,[2] twenty-five miles from Coshocton,[3] where I left my family, and went on horseback to Fort Pitt. I told [19] my partners, it was risking the property, and our lives also, to continue attempting to trade in such perilous times; and once more, made a proposition to dissolve, and quit, as the Indians had taken all our profits; but they thought I had better try, and stand it out, until the goods were all sold. I then returned to my family;[4]

---

[1] From this, it will be seen that Leith had his family with him at Coshocton.

[2] Tapacon, or, more correctly, Tuppakin, was the Indian name for New Schönbrunn, the upper Moravian mission town upon the Tuscarawas, on the west side of that stream, one and a quarter miles south of the present site of New Philadelphia, Tuscarawas county, Ohio. The village was left without occupants in September, 1781, upon the occasion of its inhabitants being compelled by the British Indians to follow them to the Sandusky. The cabins of the place were burned, early in 1782, by Williamson's men, at the time of their killing their Moravian and other Indian prisoners—a transaction generally known in history as the "Gnadenhütten affair."

[3] That is, twenty-five miles up the Tuscarawas river from Coshocton.

[4] His family was still at "Tapacon."

but just before my arrival at home, two Indians came
to my house, and told my wife, that we had better move
to Fort Pitt: they said the Mingoes had killed, and
taken all the property of, the two traders[1] we left at
Coshocton. I then left my goods and skins with the
two Indians, and set out with my family, for Fort Pitt;
where we arrived in safety.[2] Soon after, I returned

---

[1] William Dawson and Charles McClain. The two traders
are spoken of by Leith in such a way as to raise the presumption
that he had mentioned them before ; but such was not the case ;
nor were the traders killed ; but their employes, four in number,
were slain, as explained in the next note.

[2] Immediately upon Leith's arrival with his family at Fort Pitt,
he made an affidavit as to the circumstances that had transpired
upon the Muskingum and Tuscarawas, that the information might
be sent to the state officials at Philadelphia. It was as follows :

"PITTSBURGH, *May* 16*th*, 1786.

"The information of Mr. John Leith, being this instant arrived
from Muskingum [as the Tuscarawas was then called] from his
camp, he says that he arrived at his camp from this place on Sat-
urday, the thirteenth of this month ; and on his arrival, he found
every thing to his satisfaction, only that, by making inquiry, he
found that two Delaware Indians had come there above a quarter
of an hour before him, who informed him that a certain William
Dawson and Charles McClain, who were in the Indian trading
business [at Coshocton] were robbed of all their goods and property that they had with them the same morning, about eleven
o'clock,—likewise four of their working hands were killed. The
opinion of the above mentioned Indians of Dawson and Mc-
Clain's lives being saved was, that it was because of their having

with five men, to Tapacon; where I found my skins, where the Indians had hid them; but they had taken the goods and horses with them. We took the skins

been formerly British traders, but at this time their goods were from the United States.

"The same two Indians told Mr. Leith to depart from that place as quick as possible, as he was in very great danger of his life. They likewise were so friendly with him that they took upon themselves to secure all his goods and property that he had at his camp. As for himself, they told him to escape immediately, as they were sure there would be a party of Cherokees and Mingo Indians there that night to cut them all off likewise [that is, Leith and his family]. They told him that there was another party gone to the Salt Licks to cut off the white people that were there—if they had not already got there. Upon the hearing of this news, he [Leith] immediately departed from that place unto here [Pittsburgh], leaving all his property in the care of the two mentioned Indians and one more who was hired with them.

"[Signed] JOHN LEITH.

"Sworn and subscribed before me, May 17, 1786.

"MICHAEL HUFFNAGLE."

Thereupon, Mr. Huffnagle wrote to the Secretary of the Supreme Executive Council of Pennsylvania as follows:

"PITTSBURGH, *May* 17, 1786.

"*Sir:* A few days ago, a committee appointed at this place wrote to the President and Supreme Executive [Council of Pennsylvania] informing them of our situation, and the disposition of the Indians, from the different information we had received. I am very sorry that I must address you, to give the now information to Council again, for which information I inclose you the deposition of Mr. John Leith, a man employed by Mr. [David]

on to Fort Pitt; and soon after, I set out for the Shawnee Towns;[1] and when I arrived there, found my horses and goods.

I then set out with a hunting party, of seventeen Indians, to Stillwater,[2] Muskingum,[3] Licking,[4] &c. In

---

Duncan in the Indian trade. I would also mention that, although it is probable that the Delaware Indians and Wyandots wish to be friendly, yet something ought to be done, as the people that are now doing the mischief are part of the Mingo nation; and that nation [the Wyandots] not calling them to an account, shows that they must countenance them in it, or that they are afraid to say any thing to them. Mr. Duncan sets off to-morrow morning to look after his property. At his return, I will give you such information as I may receive.

" Your very humble serv't,

" MICH. HUFFNAGLE.

" GEN. JOHN ARMSTRONG, JR., Secretary Supreme Executive [Council], Philadelphia."

[1] Upon the Mad river, before described.

[2] Stillwater creek rises in what is now Belmont county, Ohio; runs in a north-northwest direction, intersects Harrison county, and enters the Tuscarawas river about seven miles below New Philadelphia.

[3] By Muskingum, Leith here means the Tuscarawas, which was then called Muskingum as far up as the mouth of Sandy creek.

[4] Licking river is formed by the North Fork, the South Fork, and Raccoon creek, which unite at Newark, in Licking county, Ohio. The river runs eastward to Muskingum county, and southeastward to Zanesville, where it enters the Muskingum river.

the course of the rout, I sold my goods for peltry, and returned to Pittsburg. Shortly after, I settled up with my partners, and gave them the horses. I then left there with my family, and settled myself on Huron River,[1] in a Moravian Town;[2] where I remained some years. About that time, Gen. Harmer came with an army, to the Maumee River;[3] and the appearance of

[1] Huron river, of Ohio, rises in the north part of that state, and, flowing through what are now Huron and Erie counties, enters Lake Erie at the site of the present village of Huron, in the last mentioned county.

[2] This Moravian Indian town was about two miles north of what is now the town of Milan, in Erie county, Ohio, and was occupied for the first time in May, 1787; but the language of Leith justifies the conclusion that he left Pittsburgh in the latter part of 1786. It is probable, therefore, that he and his family first rejoined the Moravian Indians in their village upon the Cuyahoga river, in what is now Independence township, Cuyahoga county, Ohio, where they were located when he left Pittsburgh, and where they spent the winter of 1786-7; then in May, 1787, removing to the Huron river along with those Indians. Here Leith and his family remained until November, 1790, a period, since their leaving Pittsburgh, of about four years.

[3] In July, 1790, Arthur St. Clair, Governor of the Northwest Territory, while at Fort Washington, the site of what is now Cincinnati, Ohio, concerted, along with General Josiah Harmar, an expedition against the Maumee Indian towns in the vicinity of what is now Fort Wayne, Indiana. The army consisted of fourteen hundred and fifty-three men. The result was the infliction

things wore a very gloomy aspect. I knew not at what moment we might all be taken, killed and plundered; and yet, not suffered to remove.[1] One day, while I was pulling turnips, something, as it were, said to me, while I was stooping down, "What are you doing here? now is your time; make your escape with your family." I raised up—thought a while on the matter; and concluded it was all a notion of the brain; and commenced my work again; when the same thing rang in my mind again; and on considerable reflection, went and told my wife of it. Her reply was [20] we shall certainly be killed, or taken, before we can possibly get through the wilderness. I then concluded, with her, it was more hazardous to go than to stay, and went to my work again. In a few minutes, the same reflection came again, more impressive than before. I went again to my wife, and informed her of it. She answered, I might do as I pleased. I then requested her secretly to pre-

of a considerable loss upon the enemy at their towns on the Maumee river, but at a cost, in killed, wounded and missing, considerably larger to the American army than that sustained by the savages.

[1] Subsequent events proved that his fears were well grounded; for, soon after Harmar's campaign, the savages, at a grand council, held at the site of the present city of Fort Wayne, Indiana, determined to begin a general war. This was followed immediately by an attempt, on the part of the hostile savages, to remove the Moravian Indians to the head of the Maumee, from the Huron river, to compel them to join their war-parties.

pare a good portion of parched corn, to pound it, and put plenty of sugar with it, for our journey; and I employed myself in making ready. On the first day of November,[1] we started for Fort Pitt; and on the seventeenth, in the evening, we arrived at Big Beaver creek,[2] at the American station,[3] after travelling upwards of two hundred miles;[4] every moment, fearfully looking for the Indians to overtake us. Such awful feelings and distress, I suppose, no man living, ever felt, as I had on the way; for, if we had been overtaken, we should all have been butchered or burnt alive. We remained three days at the station; after which, we set out again for Fort Pitt; where we arrived on the second day. From thence we went to Budd's Ferry; and

---

[1] This was in the year 1790.

[2] Beaver river, of Pennsylvania, is formed by the Mahoning and Shenango rivers, which unite in Lawrence county, about three miles south of New Castle. It runs southward, and enters the Ohio in Beaver county, at Rochester, and near the borough of Beaver.

[3] Fort McIntosh.

[4] This journey on foot, of over two hundred miles, in seventeen days, from a point just north of what is now Milan, in Erie county, Ohio, to the present borough of Beaver, Beaver county, Pennsylvania, by Leith and his family, consisting of his wife and two children, in the bleak month of November, with nothing to eat but parched corn, was certainly a trip of no ordinary character. Contrast this with one of the present day, along nearly the same route, in a palace car, as to time and convenience!

there I found my wife's relations, who received us with a cordial welcome. We settled there among them, and set up farming.

I have now got through with a narrative of some of my savage life, for eighteen years together, among the Indians; by which, the reader may imagine the sufferings I was prone to, during that time, as well as the savage disposition my mind had imbibed; where I could see or hear nothing, but scenes of bloodshed and carnage, sufficient to strike horror into any but savage hearts.[1]

I will now give a short sketch of the merciful dealings of God towards me, in bringing me from the savage haunts of darkness, into the kingdom of his grace, to lead a religious life. My father was born in the city of Leeth, in Scotland, and my mother in Virginia, in the United States of America. They both [21] belonged to the Church of England, and were very pious in their way; but died too soon to give any example to

---

[1] Here ends the relation, by John Leith, of his sixteen years and some months experience of savage life. It is true that he speaks of eighteen years as the duration of his time in the wilderness; but this computation was doubtless the work of Mr. Jeffries, made because of the supposed correctness of 1772 being the date of his first captivity, when it should have been 1774, as is abundantly evident. It is proper here to state that Leith died at his home in Fairfield county, Ohio, in 1832, the next year after the publication of his narrative by Mr. Jeffries.

me. After leaving my uncle, I was entirely among strangers; and thought or cared very little about re-ligion. When I was about sixteen years of age, one morning my mistress sent me to the spring for a pitcher of water, not more than forty steps from the door; while I was on the way, I was seized with a trembling; and by the time I returned with the water, I shook as with an ague. My master noticing it, asked me, what was the matter. I told him, I did not know. He then told me to go to bed. I went up stairs, and lay down; and he brought a glass of liquor to me; but I could not take it. I recollected nothing for some hours af-terwards. The first thing I recollected was, my master came to the bed with some stewed liquor; but the smell was so disagreeable, that I could not bear it, and I told him I could not take it; but he forced it on me. So soon as I had swallowed it, I puked it up again. He then turned from me, and said, "Poor fellow;" which was the last thing I knew for nine days and nights. All this time, I was in a kind of sleep or stupor; and the following scenes, or visions, took place in my mind:

At first, there was something resembling a cart, came into the room, and took me up the chimney: I next found myself on the side of a steep mountain, which, I thought, I must climb to the top; which seemed to be a great distance. Sometimes, I would almost gain the summit; when, I would get on a rolling stone, which would carry me back to where I started from. I made several attempts, until I thought I had worn my arms off to my elbows, and my legs to my knees; when, at last, by a hard effort, I gained the top. When I got there, I found it the handsomest and most delightful green I ever beheld, and the most agreeable place, I had ever been in. I walked along the green, until I came to the most beautiful stream of water, I ever beheld— so clear, that I could see every [22] pebble in it, any way I looked. I at length discovered a woman, washing at the brook. She told me I should go back again: when, I told her, I had very hard laboring to get there, and I did not wish to go back. Said she, "You must go back, and bring a board from Col. Chambers' saw-mill." I went back; but while on the way, I concluded Col. Chambers' dogs would bite me; and, when I passed, the dogs and all the family came after me, as if they would tear me in pieces; but I out-went them all, got to the saw-mill, picked up the board, and turned back again; but knew not how to get past the house; for when I had the board, I knew they could out-run me, and I would be taken. Sure enough, they did take me, carried me into the house, and lifted up a plank of the floor, where all appeared to be boiling underneath; which raised a steam of wormwood and all manner of bitter herbs, with a very disagreeable smell. They forced my head under, until I thought it would kill me. I struggled, until I got my head so far round, that I could see out; when I perceived they had locked the

door, which was made of stone, with iron hinges. I
continued in that situation for a length of time, strug-
gling for life in the most excruciating torture; but
finally, I succeeded in getting away from them: the
door flew open, and I ran with all the speed I had, and
they pursued me along a level road, until I came near
the mill-pond.   Here the road forked; one to the left,
and the other to the right.   I pondered in my mind,
which to take; but at length, took to the right.   I had
not gone far, when I beheld a man coming meeting me,
riding a white horse; when my fears ceased, and my
mind became calm.   When we met, he said, "You
have got away, have you?   I was just coming to help
you."   He then took me with him, to a new house;
and we both went up the first stairs, where I found
it a delightful place.   He then conducted me up to a
second floor, and from that to a third, which was filled
with the sweetest odours I ever smelt.   Said he, "Now
[23] you must stay here, for if you go back, you will
be abused; but I will take care of you here."   While
he was talking to me, I heard a woman say, "Do you
think he will live till night?"   At that juncture of time,
I came to myself, after remaining in that situation nine
days and nights, without knowing any thing that passed
around me.   After that time, I recovered as fast as
health could be restored; and while convalescent, began
to reflect very seriously.   I thought, if I had died in
that situation, I should have gone to Hell without

doubt ; but then, I felt sure I would get well.   However, I then resolved to alter my life, and live better
than I had done ; but, having no views but in my own
strength, alas ! I fell short, and the depravity of my
heart led me away from God ; for, through all my savage life, at times, I had serious reflections about a future
state, and, sometimes, had thoughts about dying, which
gave me much uneasiness ; but, being without the Bible,
or any religious instruction, I passed the time without
a knowledge of any improvement.   After I had settled
myself near Robbstown, in Pennsylvania, being free
from the Indians, and under American protection, I con-
ceived, that if I joined myself to some professed body
of Christians, that I should be saved : therefore, I went
to hear one preacher ; but could not feel satisfied to join
them.   The next I went to hear, pleased me well, and
I joined the church to which he belonged, and paid
yearly to their minister for a considerable time ; but,
on hearing him advance something I did not like, I concluded I would leave the church, which I did shortly
after ; but still continued in doubts and fears.   Some
months after I had left that church, as I was on my way
from mill, a woman of my acquaintance, told me, she
wished me to go with her to meeting ; when, I asked
her who was to preach: she answered, a Methodist
preacher.   I said, I should not go ; but she insisted I
should.   I answered her, that I had understood they
were bad people, and from their behaviour I considered

them devils, and I [24] would not go near them ; when I left her, and went on my way home. Two weeks from that day, on my way from mill again, she invited me into dinner, as, she said, it was just ready. I went in, and sat down to the table. While at the table, she said to me, " John, you must go with me to meeting, this day." I asked her again, who was to preach, when her husband named Samuel Hitt. I enquired what denomination he belonged to ; and he answered he was a Methodist. I said, I should not go one yard. He answered, " If you do not go with me, you will hurt my feelings very much." He being a good neighbor, with whom I was on very intimate terms, I concluded I would go, rather than offend him. I at length agreed to go. On the way, I concluded I would watch closely for something to condemn them, and make sport of; for my heart was desperately wicked and contaminated; not knowing I must be born again before I could see the kingdom of heaven. When we arrived at the house, meeting had begun. They were singing; and when done, they all knelt down, and the preacher began to pray: while he was praying, I thought—How under the heavens can that man, who is such a bad man, pray in that manner. He arose, and took for his text the whole of the third chapter of Malachi, commencing, " Behold, I will send my messenger, and he shall prepare a way before me," &c. I paid great attention— staring him in the face, expecting him to advance something for me to lay hold on; but it was not long before his words began to find their way to my heart; and while he was preaching, I concluded some person had told him my case; for he seemed to direct his whole discourse to me, and pointed out what a poor, miserable, undone sinner I was. After sermon, he told the class to stay in for class-meeting, with all those who felt a desire to stay in, and dismissed the congregation. I went out with the crowd, and left six or eight in the house. When we were all out, they shut the door. Now, thinks I, there is where they [25] carry on their devilment, and I will immediately go home; which I did. A few days after, a man, by the name of Martin, came to the field, where I was at work: after the common civilities of meeting, were over, I observed, "Mr. Martin, I have been to hear a Methodist preacher:" when, he enquired, "How did you like him?" I answered, the man prayed very well, and preached the best I ever heard, or, rather guessed at matters, for he told me things which I had never disclosed; his words, however, seemed to come with power to my heart; but, afterwards, I went out with the crowd of people; they shut the door, for some kind of private meeting; and, I supposed, they entered into all kinds of mischief and bad works. He then asked me, when they would be there again. I told him, that day two-weeks; when, he answered, "If you will go again, I will go with you." I answered

him, " If you will come to my house, on the morning
of that day, I will go with you." He came according
to appointment; and on our way to meeting, he observed, " I wonder if they will turn us out again?"
I answered, I did not know. "Well," said he, "if
they do not turn us out, we will not go out:" upon
which we firmly agreed to stay in on that day. He
preached his farewell sermon; and a great sermon I
thought it was too. When sermon was over, he dismissed the congregation, and we both went out with
the crowd, forgetting our mutual promise, to stay in;
and immediately set out for home. After conference
was over, there came two preachers on that circuit;
one, by the name of Watson; and the other, by the
name of Ferguson: and when I heard Watson was to
preach, I gave Martin notice thereof; and we went to
hear him. On our way, we again solemnly agreed to
stay in with the class. He preached a great sermon,
according to my idea; for he again told me of all the
evils in my heart; together with the many promises I
had made, to become religious; which caused me to
wonder very much thereat; knowing he could not pos-
[26] sibly have heard any thing of my case personally;
but, when sermon was over, we went out again, awfully
fearing to stay; and went on our way home. Two
weeks after that, Ferguson preached, when, we went
again: as we were going to the meeting, " Now," said
Martin to me, "why do you go out of the house every

time?   I would stay in ; but when I see you rise to go out, I always follow you." We then made a firm resolution again, to stay in that day. However, he said I was the oldest man, and he would be guided by me, as he only went with me for company : when, I told him that that time I would certainly stay in with him. When we got to meeting, it appeared, that Ferguson had been sent to another circuit ; and one Philips came in his place. He preached a very affecting sermon ; after which, I arose and went out, and Martin followed me ; and we went on home the third time with broken promises. At Mr. Watson's next appointment, we went again ; and on the way again made a firm and pointed promise to stay in class. Under preaching, that day, I was more affected than I had ever been before ; though much alarmed when I heard Mr. Hitt preach the first time. After preaching, I went out again, walked across the road, and leaned against a fence, entertaining awful apprehensions relative to a future state. After some time, I turned around, and saw several persons standing at the door listening ; when, I concluded I would go and hear too—perhaps there might be some good news for me : but when I got there, I found they were laughing, and making sport of what was going on in the house. It struck me like lightning—" My God, shall I be numbered with these !" upon which, I went to Martin, and told him, I should go home. He answered, " I will go with you." We started, and had travelled but a little way, when he tapped me on the shoulder, and said, "Stop; what are we going home for?" I told him I would never be found with the mockers and game-makers. Upon which, he proposed going back, and [27] said, "You open the door, and I will go in with you." I observed, perhaps they would not let us go in. He said, we would make the trial at all events: so we pushed through the crowd to the door; I raised the latch, and we went in and seated ourselves. Soon after we were in, Mr. Watson came to me, and spoke with a feeling, which had great weight on my mind. Said he, "I see you are much affected; do you wish to join with us?" I told him, I desired to be in the right way, that leads to everlasting rest: and, after advising, and trying to comfort me, he spoke to Martin also; who told him, he wished to join the class. Every word he spoke, representing Jesus Christ as the Saviour, seemed to sink deep on my heart, and my convictions became almost intolerable; under which, it seemed as if I was unable to bear up. After meeting was over, Martin and myself started home. On our way, I observed to Martin, "Now, we have joined with a people, who are persecuted and scorned above all others, and we must keep it a secret;" for, at that time, I would not have had the matter known, publicly, for the world. My convictions now grew worse, and appeared more awful than ever; the reflections passing

through my mind, that I had now made profession of
religion, and if I should be wrong, my situation was
worse than before, not yet being enabled to set faith in
the Lord Jesus Christ, and trust my all to him.

I then betook myself to private prayer, at fixed
places and times, (not believing my heart was con-
stantly engaged.) Afterwards, I took up family prayer;
but still thought I would get religion without letting
the world know it, but did not know how to proceed;
still thinking I had something peculiar to do, but did
not know which way to begin that work. I obtained
the Presbyterian Confession of Faith, thinking that
would give me some satisfaction; but on perusal thereof, I could receive no particular encouragement to a
desponding mind. I then heard of a Methodist Disci-
[28] pline, which I borrowed. I read it through, and
it seemed to give greater encouragement to those in my
situation : therefore, I concluded, that perhaps the Lord
would reach his sovereign mercy to me, though I had
been a great sinner; and contented myself to stay with
them, though I still continued to doubt and fear, lest I
was still wrong, and the Lord would not extend his
mercies to me; for, by this time, I was perfectly con-
vinced, that except a man be born again, he cannot see
the kingdom of heaven; and, having tried all means
in my power, to initiate myself into his favor, in my own
strength, which all failed; I, therefore, came to the conclusion, that, if the Lord saw cause to save me, it was

his mercy; and if not, my sins had already condemned me; and I must say the condemnation was just: but, my continued prayers were now for mercy, to a poor, miserable sinner.

Whilst I was at work in the cornfield, one day, when the corn was about head high, such awful feelings, with a darkness, came over me, that I knew not what to do. I at length fell on my knees, and prayed to God Almighty, to show me the right way, and put me in it; for I was a poor, miserable creature, and without his almighty aid, must be damned forever. When I arose from my knees, I felt a gleam of hope; but it soon vanished into doubts and fears, lest it should be resting on a sandy foundation. The next meeting, Mr. Philips' discourse took a deep hold on me; and after he commenced class-meeting, came to me; but I was so absorbed in thought, that I had lost my speech; for I was sure I should die, and go to hell. It appeared as if my ribs were leaving my back-bone, and expected in a few, minutes to know my eternal fate. When he spoke to me, I roared out as loud as I could halloo, and down I fell prostrate on the floor. He called on a brother and sister to go to prayer, while he stood by me; and, when they were down, prayed with great power; and I thought all in the house poured out their prayers to God, in my behalf.

[29] Whilst this scene was in operation, it appeared as if my load of guilt left me, and my heart felt light,

being much comforted with the precious promises of mercy, held forth in the Gospel. Now, methought, that the blood of Jesus Christ, which was shed on Calvary, had made a complete atonement for my sins, and that God, through that mediation, could look on me with the same love and complacency, as though I had never committed a sin in my life; and, for his merits alone, I stood completely justified before God; which gave me such a transport of joy, that the reader must imagine, for I can not describe it. Every thing seemed to wear a new appearance to me, and I could truly say, that though, I thought God was angry with me, that his anger was now turned away, and he did comfort me. I then rose up to tell what the Lord had done for my poor soul, and concluded my days of trouble were all over, for I should not doubt or fear any more, after so glorious an evidence from my heavenly Father. But, alas! to my sorrow, I have had many trials, doubts, tribulations, and conflicts of every nature, to combat with, since. At that time, I concluded I would not let the world know my situation, on any account, for, such dreadful persecution then raged in the land, that I was afraid, if I came out with an open profession, that it would injure my situation, as a citizen;—so far did my wicked heart of flesh lead me astray, from the paths of rectitude; but, blessed be God! his will shall be accomplished, and his purposes performed; for it is he that strengthens his children to fortify themselves against opposition, and leads them in paths they have not known, makes crooked things straight, and will not forsake them. I must now stop a while to compare the contrast between that day and this; and am sometimes lost in wonder, when the Christian complains of a hard heart, and many deceivers who have crept in among us, together with all the insinuating stratagems of Satan, to lead them astray; that he cannot direct his [30] views towards the Author of his salvation and hope. When we are now, through the providence of Almighty God, placed in a land of liberty, where every child of God may worship in that way the spirit dictates, without any to make him afraid, where he may call together his family and neighbors, to join in worship— and the Christian's life, or, rather, the professor's life, has become honorable in the world, which seems to receive applause. But not the case then; for they were persecuted for religion's sake alone. The soul had to fight, and bear up, under persecutions and privations, which are not known now; which has often comforted me, for, it seemed, as if a purification by fire, of persecution; and, I have often thought, if the same persecution now existed, that the real children of God would be more generally known to each other. The recollection of those times, I am apprehensive, will never be erased from my mind.

In the year 1795, about two years after my conversion, I moved, with my family to the Ohio River, in a

boat of my own building, and landed at Marietta; there
I sold my boat, and bought a large canoe. I left part
of my goods at Marietta, and pushed my goods up the
Muskingum River, to the mouth of Meig's Creek;
where my canoe sunk, and I lost all I had on it.   I
staid there ten days, trying to get my goods and money
out of the river; during which time, myself and family
subsisted on such game as I could procure from the
woods; but I never found any thing but the canoe.   I
then returned to Marietta, where we arrived on Sunday
morning; and found the inhabitants playing cards, and
shooting at mark, with other species of gambling. While
we remained at Marietta it took the chief part of my
goods left, for our support; except about one thousand
pounds of castings, which I let remain there.   I also
sold my cattle, on the proceeds of which, we lived, after
the goods, stored there, were chiefly expended.   After
some considerable stay, we set out for the place, from
which we started.

[31] Myself, wife, and two children, went on board
the canoe, and we rowed up the Ohio, as far as the
Tough Reach, when we halted at one Samuel Wilson's,
who persuaded us to settle in that neighborhood, on
Congress land, which was then unoccupied.   I concluded to do so; and that Fall, cleared about three
acres; during which time, I had to live on bread and
water; after being forced to part with my gun, for bread;
which had, many times, been my chief dependence for

the support of life. I was constrained then, to borrow a gun from one of my neighbors, wherewith to procure game for myself and family to subsist on. But, glory be to God! in these sad extremities, when even starvation seemed to stare me in the face, with that of my family also, which was dearer to me than life itself, he did not forsake me; but gave such comforting effusions of his love, into my soul, that enabled me to rejoice in the anticipation of that blessed day, when he will make up his jewels; and enabled me to set faith in him; without which, I must have sunk beneath the terrible obstructions which seemed to oppose my way. And, blessed be His name! he enabled me to contend earnestly, for the faith once delivered to the saints, through all the perils which opposition seemed to present, and enabled me to trust in him for all things. At length, through the smiles of Providence, I got into a situation to live reasonably well; and continued in that place for five years; in which time, I accumulated sufficient funds to purchase a small piece of land on Middle Island.

Two years before I left that place, for Middle Island, my poor wife (who had been deranged for several years, which was occasioned by the falling sickness,) left the world, and me to lament her loss. She went off without a groan, as one entering into a sound sleep. Then a scene of severe troubles and trials, presented themselves to my view. One of my children had become of age, and left me; and I had bound another to a trade;

in consequence of which, I [32] was then left alone ; and what to do I did not know ; but still placed my confidence on Him, who, I was enabled to believe, cared for me.

My situation then became such, that my neighbors persuaded me, it would be best for me to marry again ; and after a mature deliberation, and many prayers to God, on the subject, I at length was married a second time, to a widow, by the name of Sarah McKee, in the year 1802. She was a woman, who was, at that time, destitute of religion, but of good morals. The next Spring, I heard there was to be preaching at Marietta, by the Methodists ; and myself, with two others, set out to go there, which was about twenty-five miles distant. When we arrived there, we found a Mr. Steel, who was a preacher ; and, after the duties of the appointment were over, I invited him to preach at my house. He made an appointment there, and attended the same ; which was the first preaching I had heard since I had left the place, where I had joined them. After that there were regular appointments there, so long as I stayed ; which was the first established preaching in all that section of country. While I remained there, we had a quarterly meeting ; which was the most gratifying to me, that I ever witnessed. The work of the Lord manifested itself in quickening a number of dead souls, who were, I trust, afterwards, truly converted to God. Among the rest, was my wife, who

dated her conviction from that time; and shortly afterwards, professed to have received a change of heart;
placing all her hope and trust on the merits of a cruci-
fied Jesus; and, blessed be God! I was no longer left
alone in my feeble efforts, to grapple with oppositions;
but, having since found her an active partner, in press-
ing forward to the mark for the prize of the high calling of God in Christ Jesus.

Shortly after, I moved to Middle Island, only five
miles distant; and there, it pleased God to bless me,
not only with spiritual things, but in basket and store
also. I remained on the island five years; when, I sold
[33] my property, and moved to Wills' Creek, in
Guernsey county; where I stayed from April to August; at which time, I purchased a piece of land, in
Fairfield county, Ohio, ten miles from Lancaster;
where, I have now lived for fifteen years. And I praise
God, that I am yet a soldier of the cross; for He has
given me grace to support me through many trials and
difficulties; and many have been the combats with the
enemy, which he has brought me through, and is still
my shield and buckler; for I cannot find any other
pool, where living waters flow.

I am now in my 77th year; and anticipate, that a
few more rough storms and beating tempests will land
my little bark on the other side of Jordan, where trials,
tempests, storms, sorrows, sin, or afflictions cannot
reach me. I must say, I have experienced some joyful

seasons ; and it lifts my soul into ecstacies, and warms my heart with love, when I contemplate that the time is near at hand, when I shall leave this poor polluted, sinful and worn out body, and gain that land of rest and delight, which is prepared at the right hand of God, for all those that love him. And may the God of all grace, give me grace to support me, and lead me in his ways, to the honor and glory of his name, and reconcile me to all his dispensations, until that time shall arrive, is the prayer of poor, unworthy

JOHN LEETH.

HISTORICAL AND MISCELLANEOUS

PUBLICATIONS OF

ROBERT CLARKE & CO.

CINCINNATI, O.

ALZOG (John, D. D.) A Manual of Universal Church History. Translated by Rev. T. J. Pabisch and Rev. T. S. Byrne. 3 vols. 8vo. 15 00

ANDERSON (E. L.) Six Weeks in Norway. 18mo· 1 00

ANDRE (Major) The Cow Chace; an Heroick Poem. 8vo. Paper. 75

ANTRIM (J.) The History of Champaign and Logan Counties, Ohio, from their First Settlement. 12mo. 1 50

BALLARD (Julia P.) Insect Lives; or, Born in Prison. Illustrated. Sq. 12mo. 1 00

BELL (Thomas J.) History of the Cincinnati Water Works. Plates. 8vo. 75

BENNER (S.) Prophecies of Future Ups and Downs in Prices: what years to make Money in Pig Iron, Hogs, Corn, and Provisions. 2d ed. 24mo. 1 00

BIBLE IN THE PUBLIC SCHOOLS. Records, Arguments, etc., in the Case of Minor vs. Board of Education of Cincinnati. 8vo. 2 00

Arguments in Favor of the Use of the Bible. Separate. Paper. 50

Arguments Against the Use of the Bible. Separate. Paper. 50

BIDDLE (Horace P.) Elements of Knowledge. 12mo. 1 00

BIDDLE (Horace P.) Prose Miscellanies. 12mo. 1 00

BINKERD (A. D.) The Mammoth Cave of Kentucky. Paper. 8vo. 50

BOCQUET (H.) The Expedition of, against the Ohio Indians in 1764, etc. With Preface by Francis Parkman, Jr. 8vo. $3 00. Large Paper. 6 00

BOYLAND (G. H., M. D.) Six Months Under the Red Cross with the French Army in the Franco-Prussian War. 12mo. 1 50

BRUNNER (A. A.)   Elementary and Pronouncing French Reader.
18mo.   60

BRUNNER (A. A.)   The Gender of French Verbs Simplified.
18mo.   25

BUNT (Rev. N. C., D. D.) The Far East; or, Letters from Egypt,
Palestine, etc. 12mo.   1 75

BUTTERFIELD (C. W.) The Washington-Crawford Letters; being
the Correspondence between George Washington and William
Crawford, concerning Western Lands. 8vo.   1 00

BUTTERFIELD (C. W.) The Discovery of the Northwest in 1634,
by John Nicolet, with a Sketch of his Life. 12mo.   1 00

CLARK (Col. George Rogers) Sketches of his Campaign in the
Illinois in 1778-9. With an Introduction by Hon. Henry
Pirtle, and an Appendix. 8vo. $2 00. Large paper.   4 00

COFFIN (Levi) The Reminiscences of Levi Coffin, the Reputed
President of the Underground Railroad. A Brief History of
the Labors of a Lifetime in behalf of the Slave. With Stories
of Fugitive Slaves, etc., etc. 12mo.   2 00

CONSTITUTION OF THE UNITED STATES, ETC.   The Declaration of
Independence, July 4, 1776; the Articles of Confederation,
July 9, 1778; the Constitution of the United States, September 17, 1787; the Fifteen Amendments to the Constitution,
and Index; Washington's Farewell Address, September 7,
1796. 8vo. Paper.   25

CRAIG (N. B.) The Olden Time. A Monthly Publication, devoted
to the Preservation of Documents of Early History, etc.
Originally Published at Pittsburg, in 1846-47. 2 vols.
8vo.   10 00

DRAKE (D.) Pioneer Life in Kentucky. Edited, with Notes
and a Biographical Sketch, by his Son, Hon. Chas. D. Drake.
8vo. $3 00. Large paper.   6 00

DUBRECIL (A.) Vineyard Culture Improved and Cheapened.
Edited by Dr. J. A. Warder. 12mo.   2 00

ELLARD (Virginia G.) Grandma's Christmas Day. Illus. Sq.
12mo.   1 00

FAMILY EXPENSE BOOK. A Printed Account Book, with appro-
priate Columns and Headings, for keeping a Complete Record
of Family Expenses. 12mo.   50

FINLEY (I. J.) and PUTNAM (R.) Pioneer Record and Reminiscences of the Early Settlers and Settlement of Ross County,
Ohio. 8vo.   2 50

FLETCHER (WM. B., M. D.) Cholera: its Characteristics, History,
Treatment, etc. 8vo. Paper.   1 00

FORCE (M. F.) Essays: Pre-Historic Man—Darwinism and Deity
—The Mound Builders. 8vo. Paper.   75

FORCE (M. F.) Some Early Notices of the Indians of Ohio. To What Race did the Mound Builders belong. 8vo. Paper. 50

FREEMAN (Ellen.) Manual of the French Verb, to accompany every French Course. 16mo. Paper. 25

GALLAGHER (Wm. D.) Miami Woods, A Golden Wedding, and other Poems. 12mo. 2 00

GIAUQUE (F.) The Election Laws of the United States: with Notes of Decisions, etc. 8vo. Paper, 75c.; cloth, 1 00

GRIMKE (F.) Considerations on the Nature and Tendency of Free Institutions. 8vo. 2 50

GRISWOLD (W.) Kansas: her Resources and Developments; or, the Kansas Pilot. 8vo. Paper. 50

GROESBECK (W. S.) Gold and Silver. Address delivered before the American Bankers' Association, in New York, September 13, 1878. 8vo. Paper. 25

HALL (James.) Legends of the West. Sketches illustrative of the Habits, Occupations, Privations, Adventures, and Sports of the Pioneers of the West. 12mo. 2 00

HALL (James.) Romance of Western History: or, Sketches of History, Life, and Manners in the West. 12mo. 2 00

HANOVER (M. D.) A Practical Treatise on the Law of Horses, embracing the Law of Bargain, Sale, and Warranty of Horses and other Live Stock; the Rule as to Unsoundness and Vice, and the Responsibility of the Proprietors of Livery, Auction, and Sale Stables, Inn-Keepers, Veterinary Surgeons, and Farriers, Carriers, etc. 8vo. 4 00

HART (J. M.) A Syllabus of Anglo-Saxon Literature. 8vo. Paper. 50

HASSAUREK (F.) The Secret of the Andes. A Romance. 12mo. 1 50

THE SAME, in German. 8vo. Paper, 50c.; cloth. 1 00

HASSAUREK (F.) Four Years Among Spanish Americans. Third Edition. 12mo. 1 50

HATCH (Col. W. S.) A Chapter in the History of the War of 1812, in the Northwest, embracing the Surrender of the Northwestern Army and Fort, at Detroit, August 16, 1813, etc. 18mo. 1 25

HAYES (Rutherford B.) The Life, Public Services, and Select Speeches of. Edited by J. Q. Howard. 12mo. Paper, 75c.; cloth, 1 25

HAZEN (Gen. W. B.) Our Barren Lands. The Interior of the United States, West of the One-Hundredth Meridian, and East of the Sierra Nevada. 8vo. Paper. 50

HENSHALL (Dr. James A.) Book of the Black Bass: comprising its complete Scientific and Life History, together with a Practical Treatise on Agling and Fly Fishing, and a full description of Tools, Tackle, and Implements. Illustrated. 12mo.   3 00

HORTON (S. Dana.) Silver and Gold, and their Relation to the Problem of Resumption. 8vo.   I 50

HORTON (S. Dana.) The Monetary Situation. 8vo. Paper.   50

HOUGH (Franklin B.) Elements of Forestry. Designed to afford Information concerning the Planting and Care of Forest Trees for Ornament and Profit; and giving Suggestions upon the Creation and Care of Woodlands, with the view of securing the greatest benefit for the longest time. Particularly adapted to the Wants and Conditions of the United States. Illustrated. 12mo.   2 00

HOUSEKEEPING IN THE BLUE GRASS. A New and Practical Cook Book. By Ladies of the Presbyterian Church, Paris, Ky. 12mo. 12th thousand.   I 50

HOVEY (Horace C.) Celebrated American Caverns, especially Mammoth, Wyandot, and Luray; together with Historical, Scientific, and Descriptive Notices of Caves and Grottoes in Other Lands. Maps and Illustrations. 8vo.   2 00

HOWE (H.) Historical Collections of Ohio. Containing a Collection of the most Interesting Facts, Traditions, Biographical Sketches, Anecdotes, etc., relating to its Local and General History. 8vo.   6 00

HUNT (W. E.) Historical Collections of Coshocton County, Ohio. 8vo.   3 00

HUSTON (R. G.) Journey in Honduras, and Jottings by the Way. Inter-Oceanic Railway. 8vo. Paper.   50

JACKSON (John D., M. D.) The Black Arts in Medicine, with an Anniversary Address. Edited by Dr. L. S. McMurtry. 12mo.   1 00

JASPER (T.) The Birds of North America. Colored Plates, drawn from Nature, with Descriptive and Scientific Letterpress. In 40 parts, $1 00 each; or, 2 vols. Royal 4to. Half morocco, $50 00; Full morocco,   60 00

JORDAN (D. M.) Rosemary Leaves. A Collection of Poems. 18mo.   1 50

KELLER (M. J.) Elementary Perspective, explained and applied to Familiar Objects. Illustrated. 12mo.   1 00

KING (John.) A Commentary on the Law and True Construction of the Federal Constitution. 8vo.   2 50

KING (M.) Pocket-Book of Cincinnati. 24mo.   15

KLIPPART (J. H.) The Principles and Practice of Land Drainage. Illustrated. 12mo. 1 75

LAW (J.) Colonial History of Vincennes, Indiana, under the French, British, and American Governments. 12mo. 1 00

LLOYD (J. U.) The Chemistry of Medicines. Illus. 12mo. Cloth, $2 75; sheep, 3 25

LONGLEY (Elias). Eclectic Manual of Phonography. A Complete Guide to the Acquisition of Pitman's Phonetic Shorthand, without or with a Teacher. 12mo. 75

LONGLEY (Elias). The Phonetic Reader and Writer, containing Reading Exercises, with Translations on opposite pages, which form Writing Exercises. 12mo. 25

LONGLEY (Elias). Phonographic Chart. 28 x 42 inches. 50

LONGLEY (Elias). Phonographic Dictionary, in press.

LONGLEY (Elias). Reporters Guide, in press.

McBRIDE (J.) Pioneer Biography: Sketches of the Lives of some of the Early Settlers of Butler County, Ohio. 2 vols. 8vo. $6 50. Large paper. Imp. 8vo. 13 00

McLAUGHLIN (M. Louise). China Painting. A Practical Manual for the Use of Amateurs in the Decoration of Hard Porcelain. Sq. 12mo. Boards. 75

McLAUGHLIN (M. Louise). Pottery Decoration: being a Practical Manual of Underglaze Painting, including Complete Detail of the author's Mode of Painting Enameled Faience. Sq. 12mo. Bds. 1 00

MACLEAN (J. P.) The Mound Builders, and an Investigation into the Archæology of Butler County, Ohio. Illus. 12mo. 1 50

MACLEAN (J. P.) A Manual of Antiquity of Man. Illus. 12mo. 1 00

MACLEAN (J. P.) Mastodon, Mammoth, and Man. Illus. 12mo. 60

MANSFIELD (E. D.) Personal Memories, Social, Political, and Literary. 1803–43. 12mo. 2 00

MANYPENNY (G. W.) Our Indian Wards: A History and Discussion of the Indian Question. 8vo. 3 00

MAY (Col. J.) Journal and Letters of, relative to Two Journeys to the Ohio Country, 1788 and 1779. 8vo. 2 00

METTENHEIMER (H. J.) Safety Book-keeping; being a Complete Exposition of Book-keepers' Frauds. 12mo. 1 00

MIXOR (T. C., M. D.) Child-Bed Fever. Erysipelas and Puerperal Fever, with a Short Account of both Diseases. 8vo. 2 00

MIXOR (T. C., M. D.) Scarlatina Statistics of the United States. 8vo. Paper. 50

MORGAN (Appleton). The Shakespearean Myth; or, William Shakespeare and Circumstantial Evidence. 12mo. 2 00

NAME AND ADDRESS BOOK. A Blank Book, with printed Headings and Alphabetical Marginal Index, for Recording the Names and Addresses of Professional, Commercial, and Family Correspondents. 8vo. 1 00

NASH (Simeon). Crime and the Family. 12mo. 1 25

NERINCKX (Rev. Charles.) Life of, with Early Catholic Missions in Kentucky; the Society of Jesus; the Sisterhood of Loretto, etc. By Rev. C. P. Maes. 8vo.   2 50

NICHOLS (G. W.) The Cincinnati Organ; with a Brief Description of the Cincinnati Music Hall. 12mo. Paper.   25

OHIO VALLEY HISTORICAL MISCELLANIES. I. Memorandums of a Tour Made by Josiah Espy, in the States of Ohio and Kentucky, and Indiana Territory, in 1805. II. Two Western Campaigns in the War of 1812–13: 1. Expedition of Capt. H. Brush, with Supplies for General Hull. 2. Expedition of Gov. Meigs, for the relief of Fort Meigs. By Samuel Williams. III. The Leatherwood God: an account of the Appearance and Pretensions of J. C. Dylks in Eastern Ohio, in 1828. By R. H. Taneyhill. 1 vol. 8vo. $2 50. Large paper,   5 00

ONCE A YEAR; or, The Doctor's Puzzle. By E. B. S. 16mo. 1 00

PHISTERER (Captain Frederick.) The National Guardsman: on Guard and Kindred Duties. 24mo. Leather.   75

PHYSICIAN'S POCKET CASE RECORD PRESCRIPTION BOOK.   35

PHYSICIAN'S GENERAL LEDGER. Half Russia.   4 00

PIATT (John J.) Penciled Fly-Leaves. A Book of Essays in Town and Country. Sq. 16mo.   1 00

POOLE (W. F.) Anti-Slavery Opinions before 1800. An Essay. 8vo. Paper, 75c.; cloth,   1 25

PRACTICAL RECEIPTS OF EXPERIENCED HOUSE-KEEPERS. By the ladies of the Seventh Presbyterian Church, Cin. 12mo.   1 25

PRENTICE (Geo. D.) Poems of, collected and edited, with Biographical Sketch, by John J. Piatt. 12mo   2 00

QUICK (R. H.) Essays on Educational Reformers. 12mo. 1 50

RANCK (G. W.) History of Lexington, Kentucky. Its Early Annals and Recent Progress, etc. 8vo.   4 00

REEMELIN (C.) The Wine-Maker's Manual. A Plain, Practical Guide to all the Operations for the Manufacture of Still and Sparkling Wines. 12mo.   1 25

REEMELIN (C.) A Treatise on Politics as a Science. 8vo. 1 50

REEMELIN (C.) A Critical Review of American Politics. 8vo. *In Press.*

RIVES (E., M. D.) A Chart of the Physiological Arrangement of Cranial Nerves. Printed in large type, on a sheet 28x15 inches. Folded, in cloth case.   50

ROBERT (Karl). Charcoal Drawing without a Master. A Complete Treatise in Landscape Drawing in Charcoal, with Lessons and Studies after Allonge. Translated by E. H. Appleton. Illustrated. 8vo   1 00

Roy (George). Generalship; or, How I Managed my Husband. A tale. 18mo. Paper, 50c.; cloth, 1 00

Roy (George). The Art of Pleasing. A Lecture. 12mo. Paper. 25

Roy (George). The Old, Old Story. A Lecture. 12mo. Paper. 25

Russell (A. P.). Thomas Corwin. A Sketch. 16mo. 1 00

Russell (Wm.) Scientific Horseshoeing for the Different Diseases of the Feet. Illustrated. 8vo. 1 00

Sayler (J. A.) American Form Book. A Collection of Legal and Business Forms, embracing Deeds, Mortgages, Leases, Bonds, Wills, Contracts, Bills of Exchange, Promissory Notes, Checks, Bills of Sale, Receipts, and other Legal Instruments, prepared in accordance with the Laws of the several States; with Instructions for drawing and executing the same. For Professional and Business Men. 8vo. 2 00

Sheets (Mary R.) My Three Angels: Faith, Hope, and Love. With full-page illustrations by E. D. Grafton. 4to. Cloth. Gilt. 5 00

Skinner (J. R.) The Source of Measures. A Key to the Hebrew-Egyptian Mystery in the Source of Measures, etc. 8vo. 5 00

Smith (Col. James). A Reprint of an Account of the Remarkable Occurrences in his Life and Travels, during his Captivity with the Indians in the years 1755, '56, '57, '58, and '59, etc. 8vo. $2 50. Large paper, 5 00

Stanton (H.) Jacob Brown and other Poems. 12mo. 1 50

St.Clair Papers. A Collection of the Correspondence and other papers of General Arthur St.Clair, Governor of the Northwest Territory. Edited, with a Sketch of his Life and Public Services, by William Henry Smith. 2 vols. 8vo. 6 00

Strauch (A.) Spring Grove Cemetery, Cincinnati: its History and improvements, with Observations on Ancient and modern Places of Sepulture. The text beautifully printed with ornamental, colored borders, and photographic illustrations. 4to. Cloth. Gilt. 15 00

An 8vo edition, without border and illustrations. 2 00

Studer (J. H.) Columbus, Ohio: its History, Resources, and Progress, from its Settlement to the Present Time. 12mo. 2 00

Taneyhill (R. H.) The Leatherwood God: an account of the Appearance and Pretensions of Joseph C. Dylks in Eastern Ohio, in 1826. 12mo. Paper. 30

Ten Brook (A.) American State Universities. Their Origin and Progress. A History of the Congressional University Land Grants. A particular account of the Rise and Development of the University of Michigan, and Hints toward the future of the American University System. 8vo. 2 00

TILDEN (Louise W.) Karl and Gretchen's Christmas. Illustrated.
Square 12mo.   75

TILDEN (Louise W.) Poem, Hymn, and Mission Band Exercises.
Written and arranged for the use of Foreign Missionary Soci-
eties and Mission Bands. Square 12mo. Paper.   25

TRENT (Capt. Wm.) Journal of, from Logstown to Pickawillany,
in 1752. Edited by A. T. Goodman. 8vo.   2 50

TRIPLER (C. S., M.D.) and BLACKMAN (G. C., M.D.) Handbook for
the Military Surgeon. 12mo.   1 00

TYLER DAVIDSON FOUNTAIN. History and Description of the
Tyler Davidson Fountain, Donated to the City of Cincinnati,
by Henry Probasco. 18mo. Paper.   25

VAGO (A. L.) Instructions in the art of Modeling in Clay.
With an Appendix on Modeling in Foliage, etc., for Pottery and
Architectural Decorations, by Benn Pitman, of Cincinnati
School of Design. Illustrated. Square 12mo.   1 00

VANHORNE (T. B.) The History of the Army of the Cumberland;
its Organization, Campaigns, and Battles. *Library Edition.*
2 vols. With Atlas of 22 maps, compiled by Edward Ruger.
8vo.Cloth, $8 00; Sheep, $10 00; Half Morocco, $12 00.
Popular Edition. Containing the same Text as the Library
Edition, but only one map. 2 vols. 8vo. Cloth.   5 00

VENABLE (W. H.) June on the Miami, and other Poems. Second
edition. 18mo.   1 50

VOORHEES (D. W.) Speeches of, embracing his most prominent
Forensic, Political, Occasional, and Literary Addresses. Compiled by his son, C. S. Voorhees, with a Biographical Sketch
and Portrait. 8vo.   5 00

WALKER (C. M.) History of Athens County, Ohio, and inci-
dentally of the Ohio Land Company, and the First Settlement
of the State at Marietta, etc. 8vo. $6 00. Large Paper. 2
vols. $12 00. Popular Edition.   4 00

WALTON (G. E.) Hygiene and Education of Infants; or, How
to take care of Babies. 24mo. Paper.   25

WARD (Durbin). American Coinage and Currency. An Essay
read before the Social Science Congress, at Cincinnati, May
22, 1878. 8vo. Paper.   10

WEBB (F.) and JONNSTON (M. C.) An Improved Tally-Book, for
the use of Lumber Dealers. 18mo.   50

WHITTAKER (J. T., M. D.) Physiology; Preliminary Lectures.
Illustrated. 12mo.   1 75

WILLIAMS (A. D., M. D.) Diseases of the Ear, including Neces-
sary Anatomy of the Organ. 8vo.   3 50

YOUNG (A.) History of Wayne County, Indiana, from its First
Settlement to the Present Time. 8vo.   2 00